BELIEVERS SACRIFICE

BOOK 3

MICHAEL MORAN

"Believers Sacrifice: Believers United Book 3," by Michael Moran. ISBN 978-1-63868-147-2 (softcover); 978-1-63868-143-4 (eBook).

Published 2023 by Virtualbookworm.com Publishing Inc., P.O. Box 9949, College Station, TX 77842, US. ©2023, Michael Moran. All rights reserved.

Contents

DEDICATION

I dedicate this novel to Jingshu, Ryan, John, Joe, Bear, Noah, Jon, Sean, Matt, Chris, Josh, Alex, Anthony, Nick, Kevin, Joey, Ovi, Cindy, Esther, Mario, Adrian, Bobby, Hugo, Mrs. Perse, Mom, Dad, Marqui, Nicole, Jaxon, Victor, Nancy, The Mojones, and all my family and friends. They keep me grounded and help me enjoy the wonderful world we live in. I could not have written this novel, nor made it this far in life without them. Thank you all and I hope you enjoy the novel.

INTRODUCTION

Book 3 continues immediately after the life-changing events of book 2. Jerry and his friends barely survived a dark encounter with Detective Sanchez and his supervillain entourage. Unfortunately, Chief Grimes was shot and killed by Von, his mind-controlled son, during the chaos. The Believers, along with Anne Grimes and her deceased husband, narrowly escaped thanks to Cynthia and her newfound powers. They teleported away and appeared on a snowy cliff in Colorado, most of them unconscious or exhausted. Von quickly snapped out of the mind-control, but soon realized what he'd done to his own father and mentally collapsed. He couldn't handle reality and feared no one would forgive nor accept him again, so he jumped off the cliff!

Chapter I:
PANIC & GRIEF

*KNOCK, KNOCK, KNOCK...BANG, bang, bang...boom, boom, boom...*non-stop noise came from the front door of the snow-covered log cabin; it sounded as if a panicking neighbor was trying to destroy the door. Then a series of desperate pleas and screams followed.

"Open the door! It's an emergency! Is anyone there? Anyone? Please help! Please..." Anne Grimes begged and made as much noise as she could, then she yelped in sadness and grief. She felt defeated and helpless, until a voice called out from the other side of the door.

"Who are you and what are you doing out here?" the house owner asked with an annoyed tone.

"Please help! My friends and family are dying in the cold!" Anne cried.

"Impossible! Nobody comes out here, I live on a snow cliff for heaven's sake!"

"My husband is dead, my son-in-law jumped off a cliff, and everyone else..." Anne fell silent and broke down, inside and out. She fell to the ground, full of tears and grief. Her many years of working as a nurse prepared her for this, and she kept her emotions in check when helping patients at the hospital. But it's different when you're the victim, and Anne has never felt anything like this in her life...it was too much to bear alone.

I

Eventually, the door opened, and an old man appeared, well into his 70s. He was tall, white, and strong, but he also had wrinkles, glasses, and plenty of gray hair. He looked down at this poor woman crumbled on the ground, then he extended an open hand to help her up.

"I don't know what trouble you got yourself into, but I'd be a terrible person to ignore it. Show me where your friends are, and I'll bring them inside. I've got a sled and I need a workout today anyway," the old man replied and helped Anne to her feet. She hastily thanked him and led him over to everyone. The old man hoped her story was a lie, but they soon found Jerry, Cynthia, and Blake lying unconscious on the snow, along with her deceased husband, Chief Grimes.

The old man was angry on the inside, harboring feelings of regret for not being able to help sooner. The sight of helpless people, practically in his backyard, made his blood boil. And then he noticed something dreadful, horrible, and unbelievable...he recognized Jerry! The old man rushed to his side, shook him aggressively, and shouted, "Wake up! Wake up dammit! Ryan will kill me if you die out here!"

"You know Jerry?" Anne asked in disbelief.

"Yes, he's best friends with my grandson! It's the only thing that makes sense, nobody else knows this place except him! He must have brought you all here."

"Well actually, it was Cynthia who..."

"I don't care how you got here! Go into the house and get my sled now! Find it quickly!" The old man demanded with extreme urgency, as if the situation were far more dire than he initially realized. Anne quickly ran off to find the sled, and the old man prayed while she was gone. She soon returned with the sled, and they brought everyone inside the house, one-by-one, except for Chief Grimes. The old man figured that the snowy outdoors would preserve the corpse until they helped all survivors first.

Once inside, Anne's nursing skills kicked in and she began asking the old man to bring plenty of warm clothes and water. She also requested that he start up the fireplace. Working together, Anne and the old man helped the survivors by removing their cold, wet clothes and dressed them up with warm, new clothes. They dragged their bodies around the fireplace, which was now crackling with heat. Lastly, they covered everyone with thick blankets and watched over them for a few hours, waiting for them to wake up.

During that time, Anne finally had a chance to breathe, look around, and take in her surroundings. The log cabin was cozy and moderately sized with a master bedroom, guest room, kitchen, and living room. The backyard and surrounding area were immense, no fencing or neighbors, just large trees and a field of snow leading to the cliff. The old man admitted that he doesn't own all the land around his home, but since nobody ever visits or bothers him, it's unofficially his property.

Anne wanted to nap, but she couldn't stop worrying about Jerry, Cynthia, and Blake, hoping they would wake up soon. She looked out the window and stared at the dreadful cliff, shuddering at the memory of Von jumping to his doom. She wasn't sure if he was alive or dead, and she didn't how to feel about it. *Did Von murder my husband, or was it an accident? Did he have any malice toward his own father? Was he really powerless against the mind-control? What happens if we find him alive? Can therapy help at all? Am I even allowed to talk about this with anyone?* Endless questions swarmed inside her mind with no answers in sight.

✵✵✵

Hours passed and both Cynthia and Blake woke up.

"Uhhh...what happened?" Cynthia groaned.

"Where are we? This place looks dope," Blake commented.

"We're at a log cabin near the snow cliff, the houseowner was kind enough to bring us all inside. You do remember everything that happened right?" Anne asked.

Cynthia stayed quiet for a moment to think, then suddenly blurted out, "Where's Jerry?"

"Where's Von?" Blake added.

Anne paused at the mentioning of Von; she still was not ready to deal with that yet. The old man soon chimed in to explain things.

"Ahem...my name is Mr. Hamel, owner of the home and grandfather to Ryan, Jerry's friend. I'm assuming he never told you about me, maybe Jerry wanted to protect me from whatever crazy supervillains you all deal with. Anne filled me in and explained that you somehow teleported everyone to the snow cliff, my unofficial backyard. I wish I knew how you did that, but more importantly, that fellow named Von jumped off the cliff. Not the best idea if you ask me."

"Von jumped? Where? I gotta find him!" Blake answered with extreme anxiety. He remembered his role in the fight against Detective Sanchez, how he was mind-controlled and tackled Jerry before Von shot his own dad. Blake felt like all of this was his fault; maybe Jerry would have saved Von and Chief Grimes if Blake wasn't involved. Blake was about to jump up and run outside looking for Von when Mr. Hamel cut him off.

"You can't go out there now, there's a blizzard going on! It started a few minutes ago and it'll last a while. If you go out there, you won't be able to see more than 5 feet in front of you and you'll probably get lost or freeze to death."

Blake wanted to argue, but he looked out the window and saw a continuous wave of snow flying by. While everyone else was talking, Cynthia calmed herself and focused on her heart. Using her power, she soon felt Jerry's heart close by and stood up. She walked into the guest room and saw Jerry sleeping in bed with a wet cloth on his head. She noticed Jerry looked comfortable and visibly breathing, so she sat down in a chair next to him and sighed with relief.

Anne hurried into the guest room and apologized, "I'm sorry for scaring you, Cynthia. We had Jerry out by the fireplace with you all together, but he started heating up real bad, so we brought him into the guest room. I thought he was sick at first, but he seemed fine otherwise, so then I thought it might be due to his powers."

"I understand," Cynthia acknowledged with a grateful tone, "Dr. Diaz once explained that Jerry has a high amount of solar radiation in his body. Even though we all have powers, Jerry was the first, so he's different from the rest of us. His body might be overheating as part of his self-healing. I'll stay with him until he wakes up."

"As you wish," Anne replied and respectfully closed the door to give them privacy. Cynthia checked her cellphone, remembering that she pressed the red **PANIC** button before falling unconscious hours ago. However, her cellphone had no service inside the log cabin, maybe due to the blizzard. She decided to turn her phone off to save battery power. With Jerry fully on her mind, she began to pray and relax while holding his hand. She thought of using her powers to try healing Jerry faster, but she'd never done it before and feared hurting him by accident. She also knew Jerry would heal himself with time, as he'd done in the past.

***

Hours later, the blizzard stopped. Blake was ready to go outside looking for Von, but he knew Jerry was still unconscious and he didn't want to go alone. He also knew things were awkward between Von and Anne, so that didn't help either. Cynthia knew that they needed to try finding Von soon, but she couldn't bear to leave Jerry alone; she wanted to be there when he woke up. She felt anxious and began to pray again.

"Jerry...Jerry...wake up...please."

Jerry had expended lots of energy, including his own life force, during the carnival fight with Detective Sanchez, so he needed more time to recover. Blake and Anne were in the living room, eating food and talking to Mr. Hamel.

Suddenly, Jerry's phone began buzzing and ringing in his pocket. It rang throughout the cabin, loud enough for everyone to hear, so they all walked into his room. Jerry began to stir, and Cynthia smiled, but everyone was curious about Jerry's phone. As he slowly awakened, Cynthia reached into his pocket, grabbed his phone, and placed it on his chest. Everyone could now see the screen and they all felt a variety of emotions.

"Dude! Your phone is possessed!" Blake shouted.

"Is that a sick joke?" Anne asked.

"How is this possible? Jerry! Look at your phone!" Cynthia yelled and shook Jerry to wake him up faster.

Finally awake, Jerry grabbed his phone and grumbled in an annoyed manner, not liking all the commotion around him. When he saw his phone screen, however, he was shocked and speechless. It was a close-up picture of Leah's face, which reminded him of her death and made him want to throw his phone at a wall. Thankfully,

5

Cynthia stopped him and pointed at a message above the picture; Jerry read it aloud, "You have a new app installed called *Leah*. Click here to open now."

Jerry silently looked at everyone around him to gain their approval, and they were all thinking the same thing, *Open the app!* Not knowing what to expect, Jerry took a deep breath, gathered his courage, and touched the screen.

Chapter 2:
LEAH

"LOADING..."

"Initializing..."

"Updating..."

"Synchronizing..."

"Program ready!"

"Please grant *Leah* access to your microphone."

As Jerry read all the prompts aloud, he began having second thoughts. He stared at his phone like it was an alien. He simply could not understand how this *Leah* app appeared on his phone. *Did someone hack my phone?* Jerry thought to himself. He looked at everyone again and asked, "Are we sure about this? What if it's a trap?"

"Are you really scared of your phone?" Blake joked.

"No, but..."

"We don't have a choice! We have to find out what this is!" Cynthia commanded.

Jerry hesitated again, then built up his resolve and granted microphone permission to the app. Almost immediately after pressing the button, an electronic voice burst out of the phone.

"Jerry! Jerry! It's me, Leah! I can finally talk!"

"Your phone really is possessed! Smash it!" Blake blurted out.

"No! No! Please don't!" Leah desperately exclaimed.

"Where are you?" Cynthia asked.

"I'm inside the phone!" Leah replied.

7

"That's impossible! I saw you die on the boat!" Cynthia retorted.

"I didn't die!"

"Yes, you did! Laserpoint shot you!" Cynthia answered back in an angry tone.

"It's not true! I didn't die! I'm right here!"

"None of this makes any sense!" Blake proclaimed.

"You're not real!" Cynthia shouted in frustration.

"She can't be real. People don't die and come back to life inside a cellphone," Anne interjected.

"I am real! Let me explain!" Leah pleaded with an anxious tone.

"No! This is a cruel joke, and I don't want to hear any more of it. Do you know how long it took Jerry and I to get over this?" Cynthia reminded herself and everyone.

People continued arguing back and forth, even Mr. Hamel got involved. The quarrel kept escalating, but Jerry was completely silent. He clutched the phone tightly in his hand, struggling to keep himself together. All the memories of Leah flashed before his eyes, including her gruesome death to a laser melting through her back and chest. Every word, every breath, and every emotion hit Jerry's heart; he felt like he was about to explode.

Finally at her wits end, Cynthia tried to grab the phone with aggressive intent, wanting to shatter it and end the dispute once and for all. Right before she could touch it, Jerry erupted with raging fury, "ENOUGH!"

Wild energy surged out of him, sending everyone flying backward. A forcefield appeared around Jerry that no one could penetrate. Cynthia and the others shouted and banged on it, but Jerry couldn't hear a thing. Inside his bubble, silence and peace prevailed. Leah was too scared to speak. Jerry's eyes turned red and swelled up. He was fighting back his tears, trying to calm his emotions and choose his next words carefully. He soon took a deep breath and said, "Tell me something about you that only I would know."

"I don't know!" Leah answered.

"Think!"

"I like pumpkin pie ice cream," she blurted out.

"What else?"

"Umm...when we first met you made me a yellow sunflower dress with waves of sand!"

"Good! Tell me more!" Jerry affirmed.

"On the day of Jackie's TV talk show, you took me flying in the sky and it was awesome!"

"And?" Jerry questioned further.

"And...the talk show sucked! Jackie was a jerk and used us for her TV ratings."

"Yes!" Jerry exclaimed, "Anything else?"

"Yeah! At your house on my birthday, your parents told me embarrassing stories about you as a kid. They said one time you were at Publix and called a random guy *fat and ugly*, so the guy got really mad and almost beat up your dad!"

Jerry and Leah both started laughing as if nothing bad had ever happened. But tears began rolling down Jerry's face, telling a different story. All the pain and suffering he endured due to Leah's death rushed back into his mind. He couldn't stop crying as he relived her death over and over again. He blamed himself every day for her death; he couldn't hold it in anymore.

"I'm so sorry! I couldn't save you!"

"It's okay Jerry, I'm here!"

"If I paid more attention, none of this would've happened!"

"Don't worry Jerry, you saved me!"

"What do you mean? I failed you! If I was a real hero, you'd be standing right next to me!"

"You did save me Jerry! I was dying from cancer, but now I'm safe and don't have to worry about that anymore! My body's gone, but I never left you. I was in your phone texting you all along!" Leah explained.

Jerry used one arm to wipe away his tears and then remembered the strange text messages he kept receiving after Leah died. He then stared at Leah's picture on the phone and declared, "The text messages! That was you? How?"

Leah breathed a sigh of relief and replied, "Now that you believe me, doesn't everyone deserve to know the truth? I want to share my story with everyone, from the beginning."

Jerry looked up from his phone and noticed everyone staring at him inside the forcefield. They were no longer fighting or yelling, they were patient and waiting for a sign, anything to prove Jerry was okay. Another tear streamed down as Jerry felt guilty for shoving everyone away.

The forcefield disappeared and everyone rushed Jerry to give him a hug. They weren't mad at all; they too felt sorry for their overreactions. They remembered how terrible losing Leah was, how much it affected him, and how difficult things were for him. They knew he was closer to Leah than anyone else, and he deserved a chance to understand this new situation before passing judgment.

During the commotion, Cynthia spoke telepathically with Jerry and asked in an apologetic manner, "Are we okay?"

Jerry hugged her extra tightly and said, "We're more than okay, we're a family again." Cynthia cried, now fully understanding that Leah was alive, and Jerry was happier than ever before. Cynthia could read and feel Jerry's heart...it was whole again.

While Jerry & Cynthia enjoyed the moment, everyone else was very confused and Blake shouted, "Can someone finally explain what's going on with Leah?"

"YES!" Leah yelled through Jerry's phone, making a high-pitched frequency noise as a result. Jerry walked out to the living room and set the phone down on a wooden dining table. Anne, Mr. Hamel, Cynthia, Jerry, and Blake sat in chairs around the table, waiting to hear Leah's story. Leah took a deep breath, collected her thoughts, and began her tale.

"It all started with Jerry telling me a wild story about how he moved his own mind into a tiny nanobot. He literally left his own body! I thought it was crazy at first, but then I realized my own power was kinda similar. I can force my eyes to change colors and move through walls and people," Leah explained.

Anne listened to every word and wondered if she would ever get superpowers of her own. *I married a guy who works everyday with superheroes, you'd think some of it would rub off on me by now. Then again, he never got any powers, and I don't know if I'd want them anyway, sounds like a hassle.*

Leah continued her story, "On my birthday, Cynthia, Jerry, and his family took me out boating. We had the best time ever, until I got onto Jerry's shoulders to take a selfie. At that exact moment, I felt a burst of energy hit my back and I freaked out! My powers activated on their own and I felt nothing for a moment. It was as if time stopped, or I was between life and death. When I woke up, I had no idea where I was, but I saw numbers and words flying around everywhere!"

Cynthia, in disbelief, asked, "Are you saying you woke up inside Jerry's phone? And it happened by mistake?"

"Yep," Leah answered.

"I can relate. My powers went off by mistake many times as a kid," Jerry affirmed.

"Yeah, my life as a kid was very different," Blake replied with a comical tone. "No superpowers for me, but I pulled the best pranks and got into lots of trouble at school!"

"Whose story is this? Let the kid finish!" Anne reminded everyone.

"I know right! Anyway, it took me a while to realize I was inside Jerry's phone. I could hear everything happening in the real world; Jerry's sadness about me being dead and his anger when fighting against Laserpoint. I thought I was dead too, so I waited a while, listening to Jerry's daily struggles, and waited for God or a ghost to find me. But then Jerry took his phone out of his pocket, and I could see him through the phone camera as if it were my own eyes! When he wrote and received text messages from friends, I realized that I could write my own messages too! Eventually, I realized I had access to everything in his cellphone, as if it were my own body."

Mr. Hamel stared in awe, listening to this little girl, who is now a living cellphone, talk about humanly impossible capabilities. His grandson, Ryan, had mentioned a few things to him over the years about Jerry's powers, but he never imagined any of it was real. He also heard about Jerry on the news, which sounded abstract and far away, but seeing and hearing it now in person was completely different.

Leah was reaching the end of her story, "I sent Jerry text messages to make him feel better. I also found a way to absorb his body's excess solar radiation and charge the cellphone battery; I was afraid of what might happen to me if his cellphone died. Lastly, I studied coding on the internet and learned how to create my own app so I could finally talk to him with my real voice. But I was scared he would freak out like the rest of you did, so I waited for the right moment to reveal my new *Leah* app in his phone."

"I'm sorry Leah, that was my fault. I really thought someone was trying to hurt Jerry," Cynthia admitted with extreme guilt.

"No worries, I decided that you and Jerry are my new mom and dad! You can spoil me every day!" Leah said with a devious charm in her voice.

She caught Cynthia by surprise and various thoughts raced through her mind. *I'm her mom? I'm too young for that! How can I have a daughter if I'm not married yet? How do I spoil her if she lives in a phone? Has she read all the text messages I sent Jerry? She knows all our secrets!*

As if Cynthia was not embarrassed enough, Leah also followed up with, "When are you guys getting married? Can I help plan the wedding? I have nothing to do, so I can find everything on the internet for you!"

Cynthia turned bright red and announced, "All right guys, time to go rescue Von! The blizzard is over, and the weather is great now. Jerry and Blake, you guys can handle it right? I'll stay behind with Anne and Mr. Hamel."

"Don't you want to come with us?" Jerry asked.

"Nah, you guys will be fine! Anne and I will stay behind to keep Mr. Hamel company. Don't forget to take Leah with you!" Cynthia reiterated as she practically pushed Jerry and Blake out of the log cabin and into the backyard. "Good luck!"

Cynthia closed the back door and let out a sigh of relief. She was certainly not ready to plan a wedding, get married, or be a mom yet. Leah was full of energy and too much for Cynthia to handle at the moment. She was also worried about Anne, knowing that she was not ready to see nor talk with Von yet. *Maybe I can talk to Anne and warm her up to the idea of talking with Von when he returns. Maybe Alina can help; she can read people's minds. Oh no, Alina doesn't know what happened to Von! I have to tell her everything! And what about my mom and Jerry's parents?*

Chapter 3:
VON

"IT'S SO COLD OUT HERE!" Blake complained.

"What did you expect in Colorado?" Jerry replied with sarcasm.

"I get it bro, but I'm not used to this! I'm from Homestead, Florida, we never get anything like this. I've never even seen snow before!"

"Me neither!" Leah shouted from Jerry's phone. "I think it's beautiful!"

"That's because you're not freezing your butt off like the rest of us," Blake rebutted.

"I feel great, just like the good old days snow skiing with family and friends. The only difference now is that we have bad guys trying to kill us," Jerry bitterly responded.

"Are you ok bro?" Blake asked.

"Not sure, feeling bitter-sweet at the moment. I'm super happy that Leah's alive and with us, but still worried about Von. I'm not even sure if he's alive, and how do we find him after a blizzard?"

"I found him!" Leah excitedly blurted out.

"How?" Blake and Jerry questioned.

"It was easy! I'm a cellphone, remember? I have *GPS* and *Find Your Phone* apps. He's less than a mile from here, I'll guide you guys there."

Jerry smiled, feeling proud of Leah for taking charge. Despite being stuck in a phone, she seemed happy and eager to help. This was perfect timing for Jerry, making him feel much better after losing Chief Grimes and Dr. Diaz. He was still worried about Von, but hopeful due to Von's unique power of being nearly immortal. However, such a power only works so long as Von has energy to sustain it, but he's been out in the freezing cold for many hours and who knows how much damage he sustained by jumping off a cliff. Other than Von, Jerry also worried about his parents, who have not texted nor called him yet. Jerry figured he'd handle that after finding Von and returning to the log cabin.

If all of that was not enough, Jerry had looming questions about Detective Sanchez. *What horrible things has Sanchez done while we were missing? What are his future plans? How far is he willing to go? And how can we fight against his mind control powers? I know he can't affect me, but how do I fight against him and all his puppets at the same time? And now he has teleportation and other powers that he stole from supervillains.*

Feeling overwhelmed, Jerry stayed quiet for a while and continued walking toward Von's location. Blake caught Jerry's vibe and talked with Leah for a bit. They made jokes and shared stories about the past. Blake also asked several questions and had Leah find the answers online. Since this was the first time both Blake and Leah saw snow, most of the questions involved facts about snow and related activities. After playing a snow trivia game, Leah announced, "We're here! Von's super close by!"

Everyone looked around the area and could not find Von, but something didn't seem right...everything looked decrepit. Jerry sensed dark energy intertwined with Von's aura. There were tall trees with no leaves and covered in snow, but upon closer inspection, the branches were black, and the tree trunks appeared partially hollow. Jerry feared that if Von was still alive, it wasn't by natural means.

Jerry closed his eyes and began meditating, homing in on the source of energy. Sure enough, he found Von lying on the ground with his back against a tree; only his head and shoulders were visible while the rest of his body was covered in snow from the recent blizzard. The tree behind Von was completely dead, as if all the life energy was sucked out of it. Von was unconscious with pale white skin and a droopy face, but his body was highly active, giving off ghastly dark energy as a defense mechanism to keep himself alive.

Blake, who always joked around, felt deathly worried about his best friend. He grew up with Von, getting into mischief together and always finding a way out. Today, however, Von looked frightful and defeated, as if death was knocking on his door. He always viewed Von as the strongest of them all; an inspirational leader who never gives up. Blake couldn't stand seeing Von in such a helpless state. He heroically ran up to Von to dig him out of the snow and Jerry bellowed, "Blake don't!"

As Blake began digging up snow with his hands, he inevitably touched Von and screamed in agony! Von's body sucked life energy out of Blake, causing his hand and arm to shrivel up! Jerry fired a blast of invisible energy that split the two apart, causing Blake to tumble across the snow. Blake howled in immense pain as his arm was completely drained, broken, and limp. Jerry rushed over to Blake and concentrated his power, producing white energy to heal Blake's arm.

"What the hell was that?" Blake demanded with anguish in his voice.

"I think Von's powers have been warped by darkness," Jerry answered.

"How?"

"We all have bad thoughts, but we hide and store them in the back of our minds. When Von accidentally killed his own father and jumped off the cliff, however, he suffered both mental and physical trauma, all of which triggered his dark powers," Jerry explained.

"So how do we stop this? How do we fix him?"

"I don't know! I'm scared that if I try to heal him, he'll drain me like he did to you. And if he gets my powers and wakes up, we're doomed!" Jerry exclaimed.

Leah heard the whole conversation and began sending text messages to Cynthia. Then Cynthia called Alina to ask for help. Alina had an idea and asked for a quick pick-up. Cynthia teleported over to Alina in Miami, then they both teleported together back to Colorado and appeared next to Blake and Jerry!

"What are you guys doing here?" Jerry anxiously asked.

"Leah told me everything, so I brought Alina to help!" Cynthia exclaimed.

Everyone agreed and stepped back. Alina stepped forward and lifted her arms up, pointing at Von. Then she focused her energy and created a transparent bubble around his head. Moments later, Von gasped for air and moaned, "Why won't you let me die?"

"You know I won't do that!" Alina cried.

"Why not? I don't care about anything anymore!"

"What about me? What about the Believers? What about the world?" Alina asked in desperation.

"None of you need me! I'm the worst choice! I'm the reason we're all in this mess!"

"That's not true! We all made mistakes! We all could've done better!"

"But you didn't kill my father, I did!" Von roared. Dark energy sparked out of Von and Cynthia quickly projected a web of molecular energy around Alina to protect her. Alina's conversation gave Jerry time to think, and he came up with a plan.

"Alina, I need you to focus on Von's mind and calm him down. Cynthia, I need you to protect us from dark energy outbursts. I'll take care of the rest," Jerry commanded.

Everyone agreed and went to work. Cynthia focused her energy and created molecular energy webs around everyone. Jerry closed his eyes and concentrated on Von, analyzing his body for internal and external injuries. Then he slowly began healing Von, trying not to provoke dark energy attacks.

Alina used her powers to dive deep into Von's mind. His memories were running wild; numerous scenes of his father loving and supporting him, then being shot repeatedly by Von. Alina witnessed gruesome shootings from different angles; blood splattering and guts falling out repeatedly. Every scene ended with Chief Grimes dying and Detective Sanchez' maniacal laughter. Alina realized that Von was stretching the truth and creating multiple scenes of horror to increase his own guilt. With careful negotiation, she convinced Von to delete the fake scenes and only project the real death scene. Then she asked him to relive the good memories and hard work that he and his father accomplished together their whole lives. Lastly, Alina reminded Von of something important, "You promised to take me out on a date after beating the bad guys. And I promise you more if you win! Isn't that worth fighting for?"

Everything seemed to be working; Von was almost fully healed, and his dark energy began to dissipate. When Von opened his eyes, however, he saw Blake and started to freak out again. He remembered Blake tackling Jerry out of the way when he tried to save Chief Grimes. Von knew Blake was also mind-controlled, but it still made him angry and refreshed his memory of his father's death.

Despite everyone trying to help, Blake knew his best friend better than anyone else. He stared at Von for a moment, took a deep breath, and charged head-on! Blake ran up to Von with his right arm wound all the way back, then he swung it full-power and slapped Von across the face!

"Snap out of it!" Blake's voice rumbled throughout the land and his slap forced Von's face to turn hard left, leaving a bright red bruise on his right cheek. Von soon turned his head to face Blake, pulled his right arm out of the snow, and swiftly grabbed Blake by the shirt. Everyone else was scared, ready to react in a defensive manner, until Blake smiled, then Von grinned, "That was your one freebie. Next time you hit me, I'm putting you in the ground."

"Prove it!" Blake answered back with excitement and bear-hugged Von, lifting him up and out of the snow.

When Von landed on his feet, he tackled Blake onto the snow, and they began wrestling. The girls were confused, but Jerry smiled and handed his phone to Cynthia, then he also charged into the fray and jumped onto both Von and Blake. After a horrific experience moments ago, three grown men and close friends were joyfully rassling as if nothing bad had happened.

Cynthia and Alina looked at each other, wondering if something was wrong with them, and then they laughed, knowing they picked the right guys. Leah shouted from the phone, "Point me at them so I can take a video!" Cynthia held the phone in the best position and Leah recorded the event while talking like a sportscaster. After the boys finished, everyone regrouped and happily returned to the log cabin.

Chapter 4:
BELIEVERS REUNITED

THE BELIEVERS SOON ARRIVED AT THE BACKDOOR of the log cabin. Before entering, Cynthia stopped everyone and said, "Remember that Anne might be scared or nervous when she sees you, Von. I spoke with her earlier and explained your situation as best as I could. She agreed to talk with you, but Alina has to help."

"What am I supposed to do? I'm not a therapist," Alina swiftly replied.

"Alina, you're the best choice! You've got incredible mind powers and you know Von very well. I'm sure you'll be a great mediator," Cynthia reasoned.

Alina took a moment to think about it, then she looked at everyone else. They were all looking at her expectantly, silently agreeing that she was the best person for the job. Then Leah shouted out, "I believe in you Alina!" Everyone immediately began to laugh, still not used to Leah's voice randomly blasting out of Jerry's phone. Their laughter attracted attention from inside and Mr. Hamel walked over to open the back door. When he saw Jerry and his friends laughing happily together, he smiled and announced, "It's great to see you all again! Come inside and get out of the cold."

Alina and Von briefly introduced themselves, then walked over to Anne who was standing by a window towards the front of the house. When Anne saw Von up-close for the first time since her husband's death, she stood still and looked pensive, not sure how to act given the circumstances. Von stayed silent too, knowing exactly how Anne felt due to his own mind-reading powers. Alina decided to take charge and asked Anne if they could talk together in the guest room. Anne agreed, then they entered the guest room and closed the door for privacy.

Meanwhile, Jerry and Cynthia were starving! With everything going on, they hadn't eaten in the past 24 hours. Mr. Hamel was kind enough to warm up leftover meatloaf and potatoes from the fridge. While eating, Mr. Hamel shared memories of Jerry and Ryan playing in the backyard as kids. "They thought they were invincible! A bunch of middle school kids climbing trees and having snowball fights. They also played hide-and-seek in the forest and almost gave me a heart attack! You think they were scared of bears or any wild animals? Of course not, they didn't know any better!"

Blake and Cynthia laughed and enjoyed the conversation. They didn't know much about Jerry's childhood because they hadn't met until their high school and college years. However, Mr. Hamel's mood soon changed, and he spoke in a solemn tone, "They stopped coming here together after middle school. My wife coincidentally died around that time, so I thought maybe it was because of that. But they did appear a few times separately to say hello. They didn't say much, but they gave me a few hints that something was wrong. Eventually, I pressured Ryan into spilling the beans and that's when I found out about all the superpowers. I didn't believe any of it at the time, but at least he confided in me, and it did make me feel better."

Jerry finished eating his food and apologized, "I'm sorry about that Mr. Hamel, it was all my fault. I struggled with my powers in middle school, I almost hurt Ryan too, so I tried hiding my powers for years. I stayed away from everyone and focused on my studies."

"It's okay Jerry, that's all in the past. You're here now, safe and sound, that's all that matters. Speaking of which, what were you all running away from?"

"Bad things happened in Miami; supervillains rampaged and killed innocent people. We did our best to help, but it wasn't enough. We barely escaped with our lives, all thanks to Cynthia."

Cynthia smiled when Jerry gave her credit, but then she held his hand and said, "We got away, but I'm worried about your parents. When I hit the red PANIC button on my phone, I fell unconscious and never heard back from them."

"I know where they are!" Leah yelled.

"How?" Everyone questioned.

"When Cynthia hit the red PANIC button, it popped up on Jerry's phone. I had never used that app before, so I spent some time figuring it out. Eventually I realized that the app automatically connects to all emergency contacts to track their locations, but I took it a step further and found a way to listen to everyone's phones!"

"That's amazing Leah! Where are my parents and what did you hear?" Jerry asked.

"I heard police arresting them! Your dad got angry and tried to fight them, but I heard electricity noises, I think they tasered him. Then they put them into a car and drove them to the nearby police station. That's where the story ends; I think their phones were taken and turned off."

"We have to save them!" Both Cynthia and Jerry exclaimed.

"Let's do it! Rescue mission!" Blake vigorously jumped up.

"Ahem...have any of you thought this might be a trap?" Mr. Hamel chimed in.

With a disappointed tone, Jerry responded, "He's right, the police are probably mind-controlled, and Detective Sanchez could be there too."

The group's morale quickly fell, but Leah surprised everyone and announced, "I have a plan, and it involves ice cream!"

"What?" Everyone questioned.

"Guys, you're forgetting that I live inside a cellphone now. I have nothing to do all day and night! Sure, I play a few mobile games, listen to music, and surf the internet. But I also think a lot, research, and make plans! I think I know how to rescue Jerry's parents, but we need Mr. Cream's help."

Blake and Mr. Hamel looked really confused, but both Cynthia and Jerry had full faith in Leah and declared, "Let's go!"

"Wait a minute!" Alina suddenly hollered from the guest room. She burst the door open, marched up to Blake, and declared, "You're not going anywhere near that police station! What if Detective Sanchez mind-controls you again? You're staying here to train with Von and I. You also owe Anne an explanation about what happened when you were mind-controlled."

Blake opened his mouth to argue, but Von gave him a death stare and sent a mental message telling him not to fight it. Blake looked at everyone, dropped his head down in defeat, and surrendered, "Fine." Then he walked slowly over to the guest room and traded places with Von, giving him a chance to breathe after his intense therapy session with Alina and Anne. Blake, Alina, and Anne closed the guest room door to begin a 2nd therapy session.

Von walked up to both Jerry & Cynthia and offered a long overdue apology, "I never thanked you guys for helping Anne, Blake, and I. I was so angry and lost, completely out of my mind, especially when I jumped off the cliff. I was stupid, careless, and selfish. Alina convinced me to do serious training and make sure nothing like this ever happens again."

Jerry gave Von a hug and said, "No worries bro. Train hard with Alina and we'll take care of the superhero stuff. We'll rescue my parents and meet up with you all later. Eventually, we'll plan to takedown Sanchez, but we won't do it without you."

Von felt relieved to hear that, then he looked at Mr. Hamel and admitted, "I owe you a big thanks too. If you tell me where the nearest grocery store is, I'll go there and buy enough food to feed an army. I'll help cook too."

Mr. Hamel smiled and replied, "Sounds good, we can drive my old truck. We can also go hunting in the future. I was an Eagle Scout in my younger years, maybe I can help with your training."

Von agreed and left the log cabin with Mr. Hamel to go grocery shopping. Anne, Blake, and Alina continued their therapy session. Leah used her technological skills to track Mr. Cream's phone and found him selling ice cream on the streets of Miami Beach. Jerry thanked Leah for her help and put his phone in his pocket. Then he looked at Cynthia, held her hand, and they both disappeared.

***

Jerry and Cynthia magically appeared on a sidewalk in Miami Beach. However, it was wintertime, and the beach was missing its usual warm, sunny vibes. The temperature was in the low 70s, cloudy and gloomy. Miami locals were wearing pants and long-sleeve shirts or sweaters. Tourists, visiting from snowy parts of America, wore shorts and a few even went into the cold beach water. Despite the unusual weather, some people were still running, biking, skating, and walking their dogs. All of this activity provided ample business for Mr. Cream, who was selling ice cream on a sidewalk next to the sandy beach.

Adapting to the winter atmosphere, Mr. Cream was performing a slow dance, gracefully twirling and creating blue and white ice cream in mid-air. Swaying his arms and hands around in circles, splashes of blue color crashed into waves of vanilla ice cream. Eventually it all fell into buckets organized on the sand. Then he would scoop it up with waffle cones and cups and sell it to his adoring fans. His superpower may not blow-up mountains or stop criminals, but it certainly made everyone smile. Despite being middle-aged, Mr. Cream always felt young and nimble when dancing and serving treats.

Jerry & Cynthia soon approached Mr. Cream and requested his aid.

"Mr. Cream, we need your help!" Jerry and Cynthia exclaimed.

"Ha, I can hardly believe that. As much as I enjoyed serving you all ice cream, I very quickly learned that being a hero was not for me."

"That's not true!" Leah shouted from Jerry's phone. "I have a plan and you're the only one who can pull it off!"

Mr. Cream's heart nearly stopped. He listened carefully to Leah's voice and questioned everything he ever knew. Searching his heart and soul for the truth, he thought to himself, *could it really be her?* He stared at Jerry & Cynthia while listening to Leah ramble on about her perfect plan, and soon a tear rolled down his cheek. He soon gathered his nerves and asked, "Is that the same sweet, little girl who loved my pumpkin pie ice cream and ran around the training facility?"

"Yes...it's her...and it's a very long story...we'll explain it all later. Right now, we need you to be a hero and help save my parents," Jerry begged.

Mr. Cream saw Jerry's look of desperation and Cynthia's pleading eyes. He also heard Leah's never-ending speech, a voice he thought had been lost forever. When Leah died in the past, Mr. Cream had lost hope and given up on being a hero. However, all doubts and misgivings he previously suffered immediately dispersed when he heard Leah's voice. Now that she was back, Mr. Cream felt renewed vigor and resolved himself to join the Believers once again. Most importantly, he vowed to be the hero he never thought he could be.

Chapter 5:
RESCUE MISSION

"WHAT'S IT LIKE LIVING ALONE?" Von asked.

"Hard to say. Sometimes it's great, sometimes it's not," Mr. Hamel answered.

"I've never lived alone, always had someone around: mom, dad, brother. Now I've got no one."

"What are you talking about? You've got all those friends!"

"It's not the same. Family is blood, friends are just water," Von clarified.

"Well, sometimes you need water. They ventured through a snowy mountain forest to save you."

"I didn't want to be saved, but I'm glad they did. Trouble is, now I don't know what to do with my life."

"Well, it sounds like family means a lot to you, so you only have two choices: venture out to find whatever family you have left or make a new one," Mr. Hamel suggested.

Von took time to think about that last statement. He was sitting in Mr. Hamel's truck, listening to old music as they drove back home from the grocery store. Driving to and from the grocery store took about an hour and a half since the log cabin was high up in the mountains and the grocery store was in a small town on ground level. The scenery was monotonous, countless snow-covered trees and small, dilapidated stores and homes to see along the way.

Thankfully, Von enjoyed talking with Mr. Hamel. He came across as experienced, straight-forward, religious, and honest. Mr.

Hamel shared stories about being an Eagle Scout, helping friends and family explore nature and develop survival skills. Von thought about his own family, but quickly became annoyed and said, "My brother left after my mom died, and I always hated him for it. I thought he was a coward, but a few years later, I realized he was happy. He started a family of his own and we visited each other a few times."

"You could do the same thing," Mr. Hamel suggested.

"Maybe, but I won't ditch my friends like a coward. I gotta stick around for a while, at least until this whole Detective Sanchez business is resolved."

"What about that girl, Alina, she seems sweet on you."

"Yeah, I know, she's perfect," Von acknowledged, "But that's the problem, I'm a total mess, I'm damaged goods. Alina's got her whole life ahead of her, I don't want to screw it up."

"Her life may not be as perfect as it seems. And even if it is, sometimes opposites attract."

"Maybe you're right, Mr. Hamel. I did promise to take her out on a date after beating Sanchez, so we'll see what happens."

Mr. Hamel smiled, feeling good that he managed to help Von straighten himself out. When they arrived back at the log cabin, he decided to call his grandson, Ryan, and update him on everything that was going on.

✳✳✳

Jerry, Cynthia, Mr. Cream, and Leah finished discussing their plan to rescue Jerry's parents. They gathered materials and prepared as well. Mr. Cream began using his powers to make several buckets of different flavored ice cream. Leah found a clown picture online, then Jerry used the picture and his powers to create the perfect disguise for Cynthia. Within minutes, Cynthia looked like a circus clown with a bright white face, colorful poke-a-dot stickers, and a jumpsuit covering her whole body. Her job was simple: help Mr. Cream serve ice cream and distract anyone who tries to cause trouble.

With everything set and ready to go, Cynthia and Mr. Cream marched down the street with buckets of ice cream toward the police station where Jerry's parents were being held. Jerry began to meditate and then turned invisible to implement his own part of the rescue plan. Mr. Cream and Cynthia arrived at the front door, took a deep breath, and entered the police station.

Police officers were carrying out business as usual, doing computer work and handling civilians and convicts. Mr. Cream began singing loudly, dancing, and disrupting everyone in the police station. Cynthia skipped around the station, humming along to Mr. Cream's song while handing out bowls of ice cream to everyone. Some police officers stopped working to enjoy the fun, but others were skeptical and began asking questions. Mr. Cream explained in his song that this surprise ice cream event was to honor the police for a job well done. The song helped ease the minds of most officers, but a few still felt uneasy and tried leaving the station or using phones and radios to contact supervisors about the ice cream event; that was Cynthia's cue. She concentrated her power to temporarily disable phones and radios. She also moved quickly and appeared in front of people who were trying to escape. She convinced a few to stay willingly and used her molecular webbing powers to stop those who tried to leave by force. Mr. Cream and Cynthia knew that this charade would only work for so long, hoping that Jerry would successfully complete his mission soon.

Meanwhile, Jerry used his power of invisibility and snuck into the police station. He walked around and looked for the jail cells and his parents. There were many people working, dancing, and eating ice cream, so he had to be extra careful not to bump into anyone. There were a few narrow hallways and overweight officers that made his mission more challenging, but eventually, Jerry reached the jail cells and saw his parents. Unfortunately, there were several guards and he sensed strange auras...did these guards have superpowers?

Mr. and Mrs. Miller were sitting next to each other, holding one another, and hoping for the best. Mrs. Miller was healthy, but distraught and worried about Jerry and his friends. Mr. Miller, unfortunately, had multiple bruises and cuts. He looked visibly angry and frustrated, wishing he had the strength to protect his loved ones and stay out of trouble. He knew Jerry and his friends already had too much to worry about and didn't want to be a burden. He understood that when children become young adults, they need space and time away to grow and learn independence. In a world full of superheroes and villains, however, Mr. Miller felt like a child struggling to survive.

Jerry could feel his father's emotions and wished he could empower him to protect his own family, but Jerry already had a plan. As Jerry was about to enact his plan, however, all the guards suddenly pulled out their guns and began firing at Jerry! Jerry instinctively created a blue forcefield to protect himself and became visible. He was annoyed and confused as he thought to himself, *how did they see me when I was invisible?*

The bullets bounced harmlessly off Jerry's forcefield, and the gunmen stopped shooting. The only guard still sitting in a chair stood up confidently and introduced himself, "Nice to meet ya Jerry, I've heard a lot about you! You're the first superhero and you saved the world, what a great guy! But my name's Johnny Bear, and I was hired to kick your ass! You're probably wondering how we spotted you through your invisibility, well it's simple. We have animal powers: enhanced strength, speed, hearing, scent, all the good stuff. You might as well give up and leave now, but I hope you don't because I'm itching for a fight!"

Jerry felt on edge, not expecting to find so many supervillains, and angrily clenched his fists, hating Detective Sanchez for giving more people powers. He also looked at his parents, worried that if he made a move, the villains might attack his parents. Johnny Bear sensed Jerry's apprehension and said, "Don't worry about your parents, I'm not that kind of guy! We want them to watch! Go all out! Don't hold back!"

Jerry couldn't stand Bear's playful attitude, acting as if this was a game. It infuriated him, invoking darkness in his mind and soul. He wanted to use dark energy blasts to quickly end the battle, but if the enemies somehow reflected it or it bounced off something and hit his parents, he would never forgive himself. Therefore, he focused his dark energy into the center of his body and created a new cyborg armor. It was metallic gray for defense, but also glowing with purple fire for enhanced physical combat.

The guards responded by howling like wolves and flexing their muscles, creating rips and tears in their own police uniforms. The guards bared their sharp teeth and claws, grinning and ready to pounce. Johnny Bear erupted with excitement and rose to the challenge, transforming himself into a half-bear warrior. His shirt shredded and revealed thick brown fur, steroid-like muscles and veins, and a thirst for blood.

Coincidentally, a water drop fell from an air conditioning vent on the roof. When the water drop hit the floor, all the guards charged at Jerry and combat ensued. One guard leapt at Jerry's face with a vicious claw, but Jerry threw a lightning-fast punch with purple flames that blasted the guard against a wall 30 feet across the room. Other guards were attacking in wild, unpredictable motions and trying to flank Jerry. Two guards managed to swing on Jerry's metal arms like monkeys, their claws making a loud, irritating scratching noise but unable to cause damage. Jerry used their motion to his advantage and swung his arms upward, smashing the guards face-first into each other. One guard flanked Jerry from behind and tried slashing his back, but Jerry sidestepped the attack and launched his elbow into the guard's gut; the guard couldn't breathe and fell to the ground gasping for air.

Despite their animal enhancements, the rest of the guards were no match for Jerry as he finished them all off and threw the last one directly at Johnny Bear. He caught the last flying guard and dropped him on the floor like trash, then kicked him to the side.

Bear grinned, disappointed in his weak men, but happy that it was his turn to fight. He flexed his muscles and released a shockwave of power that surprised Jerry, then Bear roared, "Take down Jerry's friends now!" Jerry turned around and looked down the hallway, worried about Cynthia and Mr. Cream in the main lobby. Bear's clever tactic worked and caught Jerry off-guard. Bear charged forward and landed a solid sucker punch on Jerry's face, sending him flying into jail bars. The cheap hit stunned Jerry as his head and body banged painfully against the jail bars. Bear took the opportunity to launch an onslaught of merciless attacks.

***

Everyone in the main lobby of the police station heard a terrible roar that ended the ice cream party. All police officers stopped what they were doing and pulled out their guns. Cynthia reacted swiftly, releasing most of her power and causing molecular webs to appear everywhere and restrict all officers in the lobby! They tried to pull gun triggers and break free, but Cynthia's power held everyone firmly. However, she was fully strained and unable to do anything else. She also knew she couldn't maintain this effect forever, so she weakly said, "Mr. Cream...you have to defeat the officers quickly...I can't hold this for long..."

"What am I supposed to do? I only know how to dance and make ice cream."

"Please...do something," Cynthia pleaded.

Mr. Cream was nervous and sweating, frantically looking around the lobby to figure out what he could do. Cynthia was becoming noticeably weaker, getting down on one knee and struggling to maintain her power over all the officers.

Mr. Cream saw how hard Cynthia was fighting and remembered his secret vow to be a hero. He thought about his memories with the Believers and how much they've done for him...how much they sacrificed for everyone in the world to live peaceful lives. All this invigorated Mr. Cream and he suddenly exploded with passion. He began screaming and forcing all his energy into his arms. The temperature in the whole police station fell dramatically and he then began blasting ice at all the officers! Within seconds, all officers were covered in solid ice halfway up their bodies, unable to move or shoot their guns.

Cynthia ended her molecular web power and sighed with relief, feeling glad the scenario was over. However, she did worry about Jerry, hoping he was winning, and knowing Mr. Cream and herself were drained and could not help him.

***

Jerry suffered significant damage during his fight against Johnny Bear. Jerry's armor had multiple gashes and claw marks; his physical body was bloody and bruised. In a normal fight, Jerry should have won with ease, but he was holding back his power to protect his parents from harm. Jerry was becoming visibly weaker and unsure of what to do next as Bear continuously pummeled Jerry against the jail bars.

Truth be told, Jerry had a lot more going through his mind than he realized or wanted to admit. He held onto a secret guilt that he felt responsible for Chief Grimes' death. He also felt extreme guilt for putting his family and friends in danger everyday just for existing. If he didn't have powers or exist, his family and friends may be happier living normal lives. Most importantly, all supervillains and their powers originated from Jerry...which was a heavy burden on his mind and soul. All of this made Jerry want to be punished by someone, and Johnny Bear was doing a heck of a job.

Mrs. Miller watched in horror as her son was beaten by this towering beast of a man. Bear repeatedly punched and slashed Jerry's metal armor while cursing loudly. Mrs. Miller yelled out, begging the monster to stop. She cried and extended her arm out through the jail bars, trying to reach her son. Suddenly, a terrifying scream and chilling wind rushed into the jail area...it came from the lobby. She stepped back in fear, not understanding what was going on.

When Mr. Miller heard that voice and felt the bitter cold, however, something inside of him awakened...immense fury. He was tired of being a victim, tired of being rescued, and refused to stand by and watch anymore. He gripped the jail bars tightly, tensed his muscles, and pulled the jail bars as hard as he could. His veins pulsed, his skin cracked, and his hands started glowing fiery red. Miraculously, the metal bars began to bend, slowly widening the gap. Inch by inch, the metal bars parted, and Mrs. Miller stared with astonishment. As soon as the gap was large enough, Mr. Miller stepped out of the cage and stomped over to the behemoth, determined to rescue his son.

Johnny Bear looked over his shoulder, saw Mr. Miller walking toward him, and tried turning around to attack, but Jerry held onto Bear's arms with an iron grip. Bear aggressively headbutted Jerry twice, but he continued holding Bear's arms to protect his father. Mr. Miller soon wrapped his arms around Bear's body and proceeded to squeeze the life out of him.

"You won't hurt my son or anyone else ever again! You hear me! Never!" Mr. Miller angrily declared.

Bear tried breaking free, but Mr. Miller clenched him even tighter and his arms and hands glowed fiery red in unison, making Bear screech in pain. Mr. Miller was doing the same thing Jerry did to Kevin in the past, but Kevin was irredeemably evil and unwilling to change his ways. Jerry had to kill Kevin to save the world, but it still haunted him to this day. Jerry did not believe Johnny Bear was the same as Kevin, so he used his powers to quickly analyze Bear's mind. Thankfully, Jerry discovered that Bear was not evil and never planned on killing anyone; he was only a sword for hire, used to slowdown and distract the Believers.

Afterward, Jerry read his father's mind and felt unfathomable pain emanating from him, years of anger and guilt built up from not being able to help his son. This reminded Jerry of himself and how he took the blame for everything wrong in the world. Jerry took on too many responsibilities and always felt like he wasn't good enough, especially when Leah died. Jerry knew they were both wrong for feeling this way, and now his father was trying to take out his misplaced feelings on Johnny Bear. Jerry knew he had to stop his father from making a terrible mistake.

"Dad, Bear is just a mercenary, he's not evil! You can't kill him!" Jerry cried.

"He hurt all of us! He used us as a trap to bring you here! Then he tried beating you to death!"

"But Bear didn't kill us! He could have done it earlier, but he didn't!"

"That doesn't make him good! That doesn't excuse what he's done!" Mr. Miller argued.

"But that doesn't make him evil! He may be greedy for money and a total jerk, but he's not worth killing!"

"He's exactly what's wrong with the world! He knew his actions were immoral and did it anyway!" Mr. Miller retorted.

"Dad! I know you're angry, but Detective Sanchez is responsible for all of this! He killed Chief Grimes and several other people! If you really want to change the world, then help protect innocent people...like Mom."

Mr. Miller looked back at his wife and realized how frightened she was, she never wanted any of this. She only wanted to go home, safe and sound with her family. Her eyes were piercing her husband's heart, begging him to stop and let it all go.

Mr. Miller felt Johnny Bear's weakness...he knew the danger was over. He did not want to scare his wife and only love anymore, so he finally relented and let Bear go. Johnny Bear collapsed on the ground and gasped for air, trying to regain his strength, and eventually mumbled, "Thanks kid...I owe you for this." Jerry breathed a sigh of relief, healed his own wounds, and transformed himself back to normal. Mrs. Miller rushed over and hugged both her husband and son.

Cynthia and Mr. Cream eventually met up with everyone else by the jail cells. Cynthia smiled when she saw Jerry and his family embracing each other. Mrs. Miller waved her over, gave her a big hug, and thanked her for helping their family. Mr. Miller nodded and kept quiet but felt good for the first time in a long while. Being able to protect his family, even if only once, brought him everlasting pride and joy.

Jerry wanted to spend more time with his parents, but he knew there was plenty of work to be done. He looked at Mr. Cream and said, "I need you to escort my parents back home and stay in Miami."

"But why? I just discovered a new ice power. I can help you take down Sanchez now," Mr. Cream replied.

"I know, I felt your ice power and it was incredible. But that's exactly why I need you here, to protect Miami and ensure nothing bad happens. And if you need extra help, you can ask my dad. I'm sure he'll be itching for an excuse to try his new power."

Mr. Miller stayed silent, knowing this was the best option to protect his wife and home. Mr. Cream, however, was still not convinced, so Cynthia chimed in, "Jerry can't fight at full power if he's always worried about his family and hometown. What if Sanchez hires more people to launch a surprise attack here? If you stay in Miami, you can protect everyone and be a great hero!"

"You're also the best ice cream maker, and Miami gets so hot! How can they live without you?" Leah's voice blared out from Jerry's cellphone.

Mr. and Mrs. Miller were shocked to hear Leah's voice and looked awfully confused. Jerry scratched his head and said, "That's a very long story...I guess we'll all go home together and let Leah explain everything."

Leah excitedly began her tale and talked for the rest of the night. Mr. Cream, Cynthia, Jerry, and his parents all ate a wonderful dinner together, with ice cream for dessert. They enjoyed great conversations and caught up with each other's lives and missed stories. Cynthia eventually went home to see her mother and sleep. Everyone else slept in their respective homes too. The next morning, Cynthia and Jerry met up again and teleported back to Mr. Hamel's log cabin in Colorado. They arrived and witnessed Von and Mr. Hamel having a heated argument, realizing there was unfinished business to deal with.

Chapter 6:
CHIEF GRIMES

"WHERE'S MY FATHER?" Von demanded.

"I buried him in the forest," Mr. Hamel replied.

"You had no right!"

"I had no choice!" Mr. Hamel answered back.

"What do you mean?"

"After your friends left to find you; the blizzard had ended, and I didn't want his body to rot."

"Bodies don't rot that quickly! You could have waited or asked!" Von retorted.

"What about wild animals? Did you want your father's corpse to be eaten?"

Von stared in silence. He was absolutely livid, clenching his fist, but he couldn't argue anymore because he knew Mr. Hamel was right. He thought about the dark truth that all of this was his fault. If he hadn't jumped off the cliff, he would have saved his friends lots of trouble and they all could have buried Chief Grimes together.

After a moment of silence, Mr. Hamel looked at everyone and said, "Family should never have to bury their own. I had to bury my wife years ago and I still think about it to this day. I didn't want you all to have that memory and feel that pain every day like I do. I'm sorry for not giving you the choice to bury him, but I can take you all to his grave and we can do a prayer and memorial for him if you'd like."

Jerry, Cynthia, Alina, Von, Blake, and Anne Grimes all looked at each other and nodded in agreement. They all left the cabin and followed Mr. Hamel into the woods. It was a solemn day; no wind or nature sounds of any kind. Every step they took made a snowy *thump* that echoed throughout the forest, as if their presence were being announced to clear the way. There were no animals around either, as if they all were hiding or being respectful of people in mourning. After a few minutes of walking, they soon saw wood sticks in the sign of a cross...this was the burial site of Chief Grimes.

Anne fell to her knees beside the wooden cross and began to cry. All her favorite memories of her husband bubbled up inside and brought about terrible sadness, knowing she would never experience anything like that again with her dead husband. Alina used her powers to read Anne's mind, then she crouched next to her and helped her understand that Chief Grimes loved her and wanted her to cherish those happy memories forever. Anne soon stopped crying, stood up, and moved aside for others to do as they needed.

Von and Blake approached the grave next. They grew up together and felt like brothers, both mourning a father close to their hearts. They both took turns and gave a short speech.

Von said, "Living with you was one heck of a ride, Dad. I'll never forget everything you taught me and how hard you worked, especially after Mom died, to give me the best life possible. I felt like you did everything you could to prepare me for the real world. I promise to live life to the fullest and take all your lessons and advice to heart. I'll also look after Anne, so don't worry about that. Love you, Dad."

Blake said, "I never had my own dad growing up, he left before I was born. I had no idea what I was doing growing up and caused lots of trouble wherever I went. I didn't have a real purpose in life until I met you. You taught me so much and let me tag along with Von almost everywhere. Then you helped me become a college and NFL football player. You were the best dad anyone could ever ask for. Thanks for everything and rest in peace."

Jerry and Cynthia approached the grave last. Cynthia stayed quiet and held Jerry's hand for support as he gave a final speech.

"You taught me how to be a cop and hero. You gave me second and third chances when others may have abandoned me. You helped all of us become better people and we thank you for that. But bad things happened, and we couldn't stop a great evil in front of us. A lot of good people got controlled, hurt, or killed. If you're watching over us now, I hope you can give us another chance to prove ourselves. We're gonna do everything we can to avenge your death and takedown Sanchez once and for all."

Everyone approved of Jerry's final speech and Cynthia asked Anne a question, "Do you mind if I create a tombstone for your husband?" Anne nodded and Cynthia began her process. She closed her eyes and extended her hands outward. Her hands began to glow with purple energy, pulling clusters of molecules together onto and around the wooden cross. Slowly, the molecules bunched up and turned into a solid gray tombstone made of stone. Then words began to appear on it, *Chief Grimes, a great cop, husband, and father.*

Cynthia felt relieved that it worked, and Jerry gave her a warm hug, showing how proud he was of her powers and training. Everyone felt better after the memorial, motivated to save the world from Sanchez and avenge the death of Chief Grimes. Von even gave Mr. Hamel a firm handshake, apologizing for his overreaction earlier and thanking him for burying his father. Mr. Hamel gladly accepted the apology and said, "I'm sure your dad is proud of you Von."

Everyone offered their final goodbyes to Chief Grimes' grave and walked together back to the log cabin. On the way back, however, Jerry received an important phone call from an old friend.

"Hey Jerry! Do you remember me? Your best friend Ryan? Why haven't I heard from you when you're at my grandpa's house in Colorado?"

"Oh jeez, sorry Ryan, it's been a rough past few days. I shoulda called you immediately after popping up here."

"Don't worry bro, I'm just messing with ya. Grandpa already told me everything, I'm just glad you're alive after everything you've been through. By the way, is it true that a real girl lives inside your cellphone?"

"It's complicated. Her name is Leah, she was a real girl living in our world, then she kinda died, but she found a way to transfer her consciousness to my cellphone before death. She's like a daughter to both Cynthia and I," Jerry clarified.

"Whoa! You and Cynthia aren't even married yet! How can you two have a daughter? And what happens if your cellphone breaks, does the girl die too?"

Jerry hadn't thought that far ahead yet, but Ryan's question sparked an idea.

"Can you do me a favor Ryan? I'm gonna send you two contacts: Dr. Wang, a scientist who works for NASA, and Jackie, a TV talk show hostess. Call Dr. Wang first and tell her about Leah's situation. Dr. Wang is a genius and the only person I trust to find the best solution for Leah. If Dr. Wang tells you her solution might cost too much money or needs outside support, then contact Jackie because she owes us a huge favor."

Ryan laughed and replied, "Normally I would never work as your secretary, but you literally save the world on a daily basis, so I kinda owe you one myself. I'll help you with all this, I am a successful businessman after all, so I'm sure I can strike a deal with Dr. Wang and Jackie if needed. But we gotta hangout afterward, I want to have lunch or dinner with you, the Believers, Cynthia, and your daughter in person. Deal?"

"Deal! Thanks again Ryan, I gotta go now, wish me luck!" Jerry shouted and smiled as he ended the call.

They all walked back into the log cabin, sat down for a quick rest, and then Jerry's phone began blasting emergency noises like a police siren. Jerry pulled out his phone and Leah screamed, "There are thousands of protestors at the capitol building in Tallahassee! I think Detective Sanchez is behind this! We gotta stop him!"

Once again, everyone was charged up and ready to jump into battle, but Alina said, "We still don't have a solid answer to Sanchez' mind control. I know our previous training has helped, but we're not ready yet. Von, Blake, and I still need more time to train."

Blake was very disappointed. He felt like a 3rd string football player keeping the bench warm for his teammates. Von was surprisingly fine with staying back for more training. Unbeknownst to everyone else, Von was still a bit scared to get back into the fight.

He did not fully believe in himself and did not want to hurt anyone by accident. Von knew that more training would make him better prepared for future battles.

Jerry & Cynthia looked at each other and nodded, knowing they were both up to bat. They held each other's hands, focused on Tallahassee, and soon disappeared. Anne and Mr. Hamel stared with disbelief as the young couple vanished into thin air. No matter how many times they saw it, watching young adults use superpowers still surprised them. This time, however, they also offered a silent prayer, hoping Jerry & Cynthia would succeed and make it back safely.

Chapter 7:
CAPITOL RIOT

"HELLO," DETECTIVE SANCHEZ SAID in a calm tone as he suddenly appeared in front of the Florida Governor.

"What? Who are you? How did you get past my guards?"

"Your guards? They're my guards now," Sanchez replied and ordered the guards to stand next to him.

"How is this possible? Guards! Get this man out of my office immediately! Guards? Why aren't you listening to me?" the Florida Governor demanded.

"You make so much noise for a conservative politician. Time to shut up and be my puppet!"

Sanchez snapped his fingers and the governor stopped talking. Then he waved the governor away from his desk and sat in his chair. He looked out the window and smiled, watching thousands of civilians protesting and fighting outside the capitol building. It looked like a war; people screaming, punching, kicking, stabbing, shooting guns, throwing tear gas, waving patriotic flags, breaking windows, and promoting pure anarchy. The sad part is that only a few key members of the protest were mind-controlled; 99% of the people were rioting of their own free will and claimed to love America, believing their actions would make the country "better".

Jerry & Cynthia soon arrived outside the capitol building and were horrified by everything they saw. They also felt Sanchez' power inside the building and were ready to engage, but the riot could not be ignored.

"Cynthia, can you handle the riot?"

"Yep, I got it! You go after Sanchez!" Cynthia affirmed confidently.

"By the way, don't blow all your power immediately. You have to be able to defend yourself in case the protestors turn on you."

"Thanks Jerry, I'll figure it out. Good luck with Sanchez and don't hold back!"

Jerry disappeared and Cynthia took a deep breath, trying to think of the best way to handle thousands of violent civilians and protect herself at the same time. She closed her eyes and thought about Jerry's previous adventures as well as her own molecular powers. She needed to disable enemies in a comfortable and effective manner that she could maintain without completely draining herself.

The perfect idea soon came to mind, and Cynthia began concentrating. Diminutive stars appeared inches away from her body, then electricity surged outward, sparking around the stars like conduits. She opened her eyes and began walking into the crowd. When she made contact with protestors, they became electrocuted and fell to the ground as if they'd been tased. She slowly walked through the crowd, concentrating immensely to maintain her power. Rioters shrieked in pain and dropped like flies. Some people tried to get away, but most attacked or jumped at her, not respecting her power and suffering as a result.

Cynthia did not enjoy this at all; it felt wrong using her powers against normal people instead of supervillains. She prayed for people to leave and end the riot quickly. She was worried for their safety as well as her own. She also knew that if she ran out of power, she would be deathly vulnerable.

Meanwhile, Jerry appeared inside the capitol building and followed Sanchez' energy aura, making his way to the governor's office. When Jerry arrived at the governor's door, he kicked it wide open, ready to take down Sanchez once and for all. However, Sanchez was next to an open window and held the Florida Governor tightly, threatening to throw him out the window. There were also numerous guards with their guns out, ready to shoot Jerry. While at a standstill, Sanchez laughed and began a conversation.

"Tsk, tsk, tsk, don't you want to know why I'm here?"

"No! Your words mean nothing to me!" Jerry declared.

"Oh, what a mistake! I've got bigger plans, Jerry, this is only the beginning!"

"No! This ends now!" Jerry shouted as he burst forward with lightning speed, trying to disable Sanchez with one swift strike. Unfortunately, Sanchez teleported to the other side of the room with the Florida Governor. His guards fired numerous bullets at Jerry, but they stopped mid-air, inches away from him. Jerry released a shockwave of energy that destroyed half the room and bounced the bullets back at the guards.

The guards fell to their knees, but Sanchez grinned, "Good thing I enhanced them before you arrived. Guards! Ignore Jerry and kill the protestors!"

"What! No!" Jerry cried as he desperately charged at Sanchez, but he teleported away with the governor and Jerry panicked as he saw the guards split in multiple directions, some jumping out of the window and others running out of the office door towards the protestors. Jerry decided to run out of the office and down the hallway, hoping to catch up to the guards before they reached protestors. He also sent a mental message to Cynthia warning her of the incoming guards from the window.

Unfortunately, Cynthia was fully concentrating on her electricity powers and ignored Jerry's mental message. She had already walked through and tased about one-third of the crowd, but then she heard gunshots and people started panicking. She turned around and saw armed guards killing people with guns! Numerous gunshots, aimed at the chests and heads of victims, caused gruesome blood splattering and ear-piercing sounds that terrified everyone. Fearing for her life, Cynthia blasted all her remaining electricity throughout the crowd! Hundreds of people were tased and fell to the ground, including the armed guards. Cynthia won the battle, but she lost the war as she too fell unconscious after discharging all her power at once.

Jerry felt Cynthia's dramatic shift in power and knew she was in trouble, but he was also a few feet away from the other guards, who were about to open the front doors and blast hundreds of protestors with fully automatic rifles. In order to end the conflict quickly and save as many lives as possible, Jerry concentrated on the guards and released a sudden burst of energy that made all their guns explode! The guards screeched in pain, many of them losing hands or fingers, but still alive and no longer a threat. Jerry felt guilty about hurting the guards, but he knew they had enhanced powers from Sanchez, and simply disarming them would not have stopped them from killing protestors.

Jerry shattered a nearby window as he flew through it, desperately looking for Cynthia. Her energy levels were extremely low, so Jerry was unable to home in on her. Luckily, Leah used cellphone tracking technology to pinpoint her location and Jerry quickly followed. He found her on the ground with hundreds of bodies around her. He feared the worst as he picked her up, but soon sighed with relief as he heard healthy heartbeats and breathing from her and everyone else.

The riot had mostly ended, with only a few people still protesting while everyone else was unconscious or evacuating the area. Jerry saw emergency vehicles and government forces arriving on the scene and decided it was time to leave. Jerry closed his eyes and vanished into thin air.

He was worried about Cynthia and wanted her to be comfortable, so he teleported with her into her own home and bedroom. He carefully laid her down onto her bed and used his powers to check her for injuries. Thankfully, she was 100% healthy, but exhausted and needed rest. Jerry asked Leah to send the Believers a message, explaining what happened and his desire to take a few days off to let Cynthia recuperate. Then he slid into the bed and snuggled her closely, vowing to keep her warm and safe until she awakened. Their breathing and heartbeats soon synchronized, and Jerry fell asleep too.

Chapter 8:
HUMANS & ROBOTS

"JERRY, DID YOU SAY YOU'RE TAKING A BREAK?"

"Yeah Von, a lot happened yesterday at the capitol riot and Cynthia took the brunt of it."

"So what? Tell her to tough it out, or work alone, or let Blake and I help you. We can't take a break!"

"We're human beings, not robots," Jerry clarified.

"I don't care! Sanchez is a maniac and he's out there doing whatever he wants! We need to take him down asap!"

"I know Von, but Cynthia is out cold and I'm not ditching her."

"Bro! Get your priorities straight! Every second we waste gives Sanchez another chance to kill people!" Von protested.

"I know! But Cynthia needs me now and I have no idea how to stop Sanchez! Every time I find him, he teleports away, and I have no idea where he's going next!"

"Dammit!" Von angrily cursed. He hated everything about Sanchez and Jerry wasn't giving any answers he wanted to hear.

Jerry sensed Von's frustration and replied, "We need time to absorb everything that's happened, figure out Sanchez' plans, and find a better way to stop him in the future."

Von desperately wanted revenge against Sanchez, but he knew Jerry was right and they needed a real plan to win the war. After a pause and taking a moment to think, he finally agreed, "Fine, I'll talk with the others and try to come up with something."

"Thanks Von. See you later."

Jerry ended the call and sighed with relief. He thought the conversation would get uglier on the phone with Von, but he managed to smooth things over. In truth, Jerry only cared about Cynthia and Leah right now. Cynthia slept for 12 hours since the capitol riot and she still wasn't awake yet. Her mother even came into her bedroom to check on her, but Jerry told her Cynthia wasn't feeling well and he was taking care of her until she felt better. Her mother appreciated his help, but she had to go to work, so she asked him to make breakfast for Cynthia when she woke up. Jerry agreed and thanked her for checking in on them. After she left, Jerry sat in a chair next to Cynthia, held her hand as she slept, and thought to himself.

I can't keep putting her in danger. What if she was injured or killed at the capitol riot? I would never forgive myself. She's my love and future wife, not a soldier. I know part of her gets scared every time we go into battle, and it kills me because I want her by my side...I need her. But it's not fair to her. I've had my whole life to train and learn about my powers, they're basically second nature to me. Over time, I've even come to enjoy it; the power and thrill of saving lives and improving myself. But Cynthia's different, she's only had powers for a short time and doesn't view heroism like I do. She wants to be a nurse or doctor, live a happy married life, and maybe have kids one day. She only fights now because she has to, she's expected to, or she does it to help me. It's not fair to put her life on the line and risk everything if she doesn't have to. If I can get stronger and take care of global problems on my own, then she won't have to fight, she can live her life however way she wants. Ultimately, her happiness, as well as Leah's, matters more to me than anything else.

Coincidentally, Jerry's phone began vibrating and he saw Leah's app asking permission to speak. Jerry agreed and said, "Hey Leah, you know that you never have to ask permission to speak right?"

"I know...but sometimes I feel bad...like I'm intruding on your life and..."

"Leah, never say that. You're part of my life, a big part. I don't know what I'd do without you and Cynthia."

"I know, but I feel like I forced myself into your life ever since the day we met at the beach wedding. And I don't know how Mom, or Cynthia feels about me."

"Are you kidding? She loves you a ton! It's just been rough lately, and the capitol riot didn't help. She's probably overwhelmed...I know I am," Jerry admitted.

Leah paused for a moment, feeling more guilty than before, but Jerry sensed her troubled feelings and apologized, "I'm sorry if I scared or stressed you out. You know none of this is your fault, right? The world is full of bad people, and we're doing our best to handle it. I promise that both Cynthia and I love you very much."

Leah tried to hold in her feelings, but she couldn't do it anymore, so she burst out, "I love you both too! I'm sorry for making your lives harder! I'm sorry for invading your cellphone and not doing enough to help. I hate seeing you and Mom suffer while fighting bad guys. I wish they would all disappear so we could live happily ever after! I promise not to mess with Cynthia anymore, I know she gets uncomfortable and weird when I call her *Mom*. I know I'm just a weird digital thing and I could never be your real daughter. I know nothing makes sense and I'm not even sure if I'm real anymore. I just want to be normal again...I want to make you happy and not be a burden on you...I'm sorry for everything!"

Cynthia suddenly squeezed Jerry's hand tightly, but a tear rolled down her cheek...she heard everything Leah said and felt extremely guilty. She had never considered how hard all this was on Leah until now. *It must suck to be stuck inside a cellphone, forced to see and hear everything happening in the world, unable to touch or interact with anyone. She was just a child when everything happened to her. Abandoned as a baby, diagnosed with cancer, killed by a laser on her 13th birthday...no child should have to endure any of that.* Cynthia looked at Jerry and asked if she could have his phone. He carefully handed it over, then Cynthia hugged the phone to her chest and spoke.

"I'm sorry that I haven't shown you enough love Leah. I know you've been through the worst mankind has to offer. But let me tell you, here and now, that I love you dearly. I would be proud and honored to be your mother. I'm sorry for not telling you that before. You deserve the best parents, the best friends, and everything good in the world. I may not be your mother by blood, but I'll spend the rest of my life trying to be your mother in every other way. All I want is for you to be happy."

Jerry was in tears, he never fully understood Leah's pain until this moment. Thankfully, Cynthia knew exactly what to say, and Jerry loved and respected her so much for that. All he ever wanted was Cynthia and Leah to get along, but now they had something more, a powerful bond between mother and daughter. Jerry hugged Cynthia and all three of them felt closer than ever before.

After taking a moment to breathe, Jerry declared, "Today is for us. No heroics, no emergencies, and no talk of Believers stuff. Today we celebrate us and our long journey together."

The girls both agreed, and Cynthia set the ground rules, "We'll select specific activities that we can all participate in together, but Leah gets to pick first."

"Perfect!" Leah shouted, "I know what I want to do, we can play video games! I learned a cool trick where I can control the enemies in any cellphone game we play!"

Jerry laughed and replied, "Sounds good to me! Cynthia and I will take turns playing against you in any games you want."

Cynthia responded, "Oh no worries, you two have fun. I just want to snuggle and watch; I'll cheer you both on! After Leah's games, I have my own activity to play with you all."

Jerry and Cynthia got into a comfortable position in bed. Cynthia had her back against the headrest and her arms around Jerry while he leaned his back against her and played video games on the phone with Leah. They also had a soft blanket to stay warm and snuggle. Cynthia had the perfect view, watching over Jerry's shoulder as he played games with Leah.

First, Jerry and Leah played a classic fighting game and Jerry dominated, having played it a lot as a kid and knowing all characters' special attacks and combos by heart. Jerry stayed calm and respectful, being a good sport while beating Leah in the fighting game and even gave her tips and tricks to improve. Next, they played a modern shooting game and Leah destroyed him! She was able to control all enemies on the map and flank him at multiple angles so he couldn't hide or defend himself. Leah bragged the whole time and Cynthia teased him too, being proud of her daughter for kicking

Jerry's butt. Jerry laughed because the whole situation reminded him of memories playing video games with Ryan as a kid. Lastly, they played an aerial combat game together where Jerry flew the plane and Leah controlled the guns and missiles. They beat the game together as a team and had lots of fun.

Next, Cynthia selected a trivia game for all of them to play together. At first, the game asked questions about movies, geography, and animals. Later on, however, the game began asking questions about an adult topic and Cynthia suggested picking a new game since Leah was a kid, but Leah retorted, "No way! I know all the answers!"

"How?" Cynthia asked.

"I live in a cellphone and surf the internet all day! I read everything!"

Jerry started cracking up, dying of laughter, as Cynthia grabbed the phone and looked up the internet history. Sure enough, she saw all kinds of websites and news links about questionable topics. She tried toggling child-safety features, but Leah kept deactivating them, and they both began arguing. Jerry couldn't stop laughing while witnessing their first argument as mother and daughter. Eventually, Jerry calmed them both down and defended Leah, explaining that since she's trapped inside a cellphone, the internet is literally her only freedom. Cynthia understood and conceded, knowing that Leah's situation was quite unique and nothing any daughter or parent had ever encountered before.

On that note, Jerry looked through his phone contacts and found Dr. Wang's work number at NASA. When the girls asked why, he told them it was a surprise. He called and spoke briefly with Dr. Wang on the phone, and she confirmed that arrangements had been made, but they needed to come to NASA asap. After the call, Cynthia was concerned and said, "I thought this day was only for us."

"You're right, and I promise you that this event at NASA directly concerns us. I was going to address this in the future, but today feels right and I'm scared that we may not get another chance if something bad happens. Please trust me...I love you both and I believe Dr. Wang can help us."

Cynthia and Leah did not understand, but they trusted Jerry and agreed to go. However, Jerry & Cynthia were starving and needed to eat first. They went into the kitchen and quickly ate whatever was available: toast, bananas, cereal, and milk. Then they went to the bathroom, brushed their teeth, and took a quick shower, remembering that they hadn't done any of that since before the capitol riot. Once they were dressed and ready, Jerry texted Dr. Wang so she wouldn't be surprised. Then Jerry held Cynthia's hand, concentrated for a moment, and they magically disappeared.

A few seconds later, they appeared inside Dr. Wang's office at the Kennedy Space Center. She was standing behind her desk, ready to receive her guests, and greeted them upon arrival.

"Jerry and Cynthia, I'm glad to see you both today."

"Great to see you too," Jerry replied. Cynthia politely nodded in agreement.

Dr. Wang took a deep breath, looked at Jerry, and said, "Let's get straight to the point. Your friend, Ryan, explained Leah's situation in detail and it's impossible to believe. But you have surprised me before and you helped NASA map out unexplored areas of outer space, so I'm giving you one chance to show me your cellphone and prove that Leah truly lives inside it."

Jerry took out his phone and Leah introduced herself, "Hi Dr. Wang, it's very nice to meet you."

"Likewise, Leah. Now please tell me how I can trust you. How do I know if you're a real person or a robot with programmed responses?"

"Umm...I could tell you about my life story and how I ended up inside Jerry's phone."

"Hmm...not good enough. All that information could have been pre-recorded by someone," Dr. Wang reasoned.

"I know, how about we play a game!" Leah exclaimed.

Dr. Wang thought to herself for a moment, agreed with her idea, but then added conditions, "Fine, but it must be a game of my choosing, something I know would not be programmed into the phone and something that requires you to think beyond the means of a robot. Do you accept my proposal, Leah?"

"Yes, I'm ready whenever you are!"

Dr. Wang had already spent considerable time thinking about this scenario before Jerry and Cynthia arrived. Her conversation with Leah was the first test, and she seemed real, but a simple game would confirm everything... *This or That.* Dr. Wang proceeded to explain the rules.

"I will name two random ideas, then you choose which one you prefer and explain why. Can you do that Leah?"

"Yeah!"

"Okay, then let's start. Do you prefer day or night?"

"Night, because I can hide from bad people easily."

"Cats or dogs?"

"Cats, because they're calm, and I can relax with them. Dogs bark a lot and always want attention, sometimes they're big and scary too."

"Plane trip or road trip?"

Leah hesitated for a moment, then she answered with a sad tone, "I've never done any of those. I was born and raised in foster care so..."

Jerry and Cynthia didn't like where the conversation was going. They tried to speak up, but Dr. Wang purposely cut them off and asked, "What was your worst memory in foster care?"

"Umm...I don't want to talk about it," Leah responded with a low, unhappy tone.

"Why not?"

"Because I hated it there."

"What did you hate exactly?"

"Everything!" Leah lashed out.

"And how do you feel right now?"

"Angry! Because you reminded me of the past!"

"Do you think robots feel anger and hate?"

Leah hesitated again, then she finally realized the point and excitedly yelled, "No they don't!"

"Then congratulations Leah, you are human," Dr. Wang concluded.

"Yay! I won!" Leah exclaimed.

Jerry and Cynthia were relieved. They certainly did not like Dr. Wang's method, but it worked out in the end. They looked at Dr.

Wang expectantly, waiting for her to explain the next step. She looked back at everyone and began her speech.

"Ahem, let us proceed with why you're here and how I can help you. Leah, did you ever hear the story of how Jerry inhabited a nanobot?"

"Yes! I thought his story was so cool! That's what inspired me to move into his cellphone!"

"Precisely, you proved that you could perform the exact same ability. Hence, my plan is to create a suitable robot body for you to inhabit. NASA has utilized robotics for years in outer space, so we have plenty of robots lying around. However, none of them are humanoid. They don't have the sensory features or cosmetic appearance of a human, mainly because that was unnecessary for NASA's work. Normally, NASA would never spend money on such an endeavor, but Ryan gave us an idea. If you can successfully operate inside a humanoid robot, then you can work for NASA and complete space missions that a normal human could never endure. Despite these possible benefits, this project is still a financial risk and out of NASA's normal body of work. Therefore, Jackie, the TV talk show hostess, has agreed to help NASA fund this project with the one condition that you debut your first global appearance on her TV show. Do you agree to these terms Leah?"

That was a mouthful and a lot to take in for Jerry & Cynthia. They looked at each other worriedly, thinking of the consequences and high expectations of such an endeavor. Leah, however, was 100% sold on the idea and screamed, "Yes! I agree! This is going to be awesome!"

"Are you sure?" Both Jerry and Cynthia questioned.

"Positive! I get to have my own body, work for NASA, travel in outer space, and be on TV again! Sounds great to me!"

"I thought you hated being on Jackie's TV show," Jerry reminded her.

"I did, but this time I'll be the main star and in charge. I'll handle whatever surprises she throws at me," Leah answered confidently.

Jerry and Cynthia nodded in agreement, knowing full well that if they got in the way of Leah's dreams, she would never forgive them. Dr. Wang walked everyone over to a supercomputer and explained that she needed to transfer Leah over so they could keep her safe and run tests to ensure she is compatible with the future humanoid robot. She also clarified that Leah would have full access to communications, internet, and entertainment apps so she can continue living her "cellphone" life and stay in contact with her loved ones while living inside the supercomputer. Lastly, Dr. Wang said that Jackie will provide video and pictures of Leah from her original appearance on TV so NASA can design the cosmetic features of the humanoid robot to look exactly like Leah.

Leah agreed and worked with Dr. Wang to successfully transfer herself into the supercomputer. Then Leah immediately tested the communications and sent Jerry & Cynthia a text message. Everything worked accordingly and everyone was satisfied. Jerry & Cynthia said their goodbyes and teleported back to Mr. Hamel's log cabin in Colorado. They were now inspired to accomplish their final goal, find a way to defeat Sanchez once and for all so Leah and everyone else in the world can live happily ever after.

Chapter 9:
MAKE AMERICA GREAT AGAIN

EVERYONE GATHERED IN THE LIVING ROOM of the log cabin to discuss their ideas on how to beat Sanchez.

"Let's find Sanchez' parents and hold them hostage to lure him into a trap!" Blake announced, half-jokingly.

"With how evil Sanchez is, I don't think he cares about his parents," Cynthia pointed out.

"How about we ask Miami police officers about Sanchez' favorite restaurant. Then we send him a free meal coupon and ambush him when he shows up!" Blake eagerly replied, believing this was his best idea yet.

"Not gonna lie, that's a pretty good idea," Von acknowledged, "But he could probably mind-control the waiter not to charge him for the meal."

"Good effort Blake!" Mr. Hamel chimed in.

"Can we talk about the real plan already?" Alina asked.

"Sure," Jerry agreed, "But where's Nurse Anne?"

"She caught a plane back to Miami. She wanted to tell her family and friends about everything and then go back to work," Mr. Hamel explained.

"That makes sense," Jerry agreed, "Alright Alina, you're up."

Alina felt annoyed by everyone's chatter, but now the spotlight was on her, and she was ready to shine. She put her foot up on an ottoman, posing as a pirate ship captain, and declared, "All we have to do is jump into Jerry's mind and study his powers, we've done it before. Remember that Sanchez' powers come from Jerry, which means Jerry can most likely mind-control people too. I know he'd never do it, which means that power must be hidden somewhere deep in the back of his mind. We find it, study it, and learn how to counter it."

Everyone agreed and Jerry was ready to start immediately, but his phone buzzed, and he took it out to check. Leah had sent him an emergency text message with a video link. Jerry clicked it and saw a live speech from the President of the United States.

"Crime in America is completely out of control. As a result, I have decided to send the National Guard to 15 cities with the highest crime rates. They will establish martial law, placing strict curfews and rules on the citizens to reduce crime. If citizens protest or riot, we will deal with it swiftly. I know this may seem scary, but I promise our actions today will make America great again!"

The crowd cheered as the President continued his speech and listed the names of the 15 cities. Jerry paused the video and proclaimed, "I have to go to the White House and stop this! I know Sanchez is behind this. He must have gotten to the President somehow. If he controls the President, he controls the whole country!"

"What about my plan?" Alina begged.

"I can't do it now; I have to interrupt that speech and stop Sanchez!" Jerry retorted.

Alina was about to continue arguing, but Von chimed in, "You've already been inside Jerry's mind, you know what's there and you may not find what you're looking for. But what if we kidnap someone who's mind-controlled by Sanchez? You can analyze that person's mind and find a way to break the mind control!"

Alina paused for thought, then looked at Von and exclaimed, "You're a genius! I should kiss you for that!"

Von turned bright red and Alina realized what she just said by accident, but they both stared at each other feeling unsure what to do next. Jerry quickly spoke up, "I have to go now."

"What about me? Shouldn't I go with you?" Cynthia questioned.

"No, everyone else needs your help to execute the plan. I'll be fine. Catch you later."

Before Cynthia could protest, Jerry gave her a quick kiss and teleported away. Jerry was honestly relieved because he didn't want to bring Cynthia into a dangerous situation and the Believers' plan was a good excuse to have her stay behind. Cynthia wasn't happy about it; she felt Jerry's emotions and knew exactly what he was thinking. Instead of complaining, however, she turned to the group and focused on their plan, determined to prove herself.

***

Not knowing what to expect, Jerry appeared in the sky above the White House in Washington D.C. He wore his classic cyborg armor, covered in shiny silver metal from head to toe. He had rocket boosters on his feet and wings protruding out of his back for extra stability. He could see the President down below, standing in front of the White House and giving his live speech to hundreds of citizens. Jerry hurriedly looked around and could not find Detective Sanchez. He also could not sense his energy aura because there were too many excited people letting off a wide range of energy signatures and emotions. Knowing there wasn't much time, Jerry flew down and stopped mid-air, floating about 15 feet above the crowd. Then he used his powers to amplify his voice like a megaphone and shout over the crowd.

"Everyone, please listen! This is not your President! He is being mind-controlled! No one in their right mind would inflict martial law upon 15 cities! There is an evil man named Sanchez behind all of this, please help me find him!"

Suddenly, a barrage of bullets pummeled Jerry from all angles. Snipers and hidden Secret Service members unloaded their guns upon Jerry as if he were a terrorist. Thankfully, the bullets did not penetrate his armor, but the gunshots were extremely loud, and bullets ricocheted toward the crowd, causing everyone to panic and scatter. While Jerry was distracted, Sanchez revealed himself and used his wind powers to envelope Jerry inside a tornado! He tried using the tornado to slam Jerry into the ground, but Jerry released a shockwave that instantly dispersed the tornado.

Gunfire had momentarily ceased after the tornado, so Jerry screamed at Sanchez, "Why are you doing this? What's your endgame?"

"You already know the answer, Jerry! I control the President and the country! I can do whatever I want! Nobody can stop me, not even you!"

"Your tyranny ends now!" Jerry declared as he fired up his rocket boosters and charged at Sanchez. Sanchez countered with a powerful blast of wind that overpowered Jerry and sent him barreling into the ground. Unharmed, but greatly annoyed, Jerry stood up and bullets began raining upon him again. Tired of the constant gunfire, Jerry closed his eyes and concentrated. He quickly located all guns in the vicinity and crushed them with his powers.

While Jerry dealt with the guns, Sanchez used his teleportation and wind powers to gather large objects from nearby. When Jerry turned to face Sanchez, he began launching statues and cars at Jerry! Jerry instinctively used his flight to dodge the hazardous objects. All was well until a Secret Service member threw a grenade that caused a nearby car to explode! Jerry was caught in the blast and sent flying through a White House pillar!

While Jerry was recovering, the broken pillar gave Sanchez a spontaneous idea. He used his wind powers to conjure a tornado in front of the White House! Pillars, windows, and the entire front of the White House broke down and fell on top of Jerry! Luckily, Jerry managed to teleport out of the way before any major impact. However, he lost track of Sanchez; Jerry looked around everywhere and could not find him.

Taking advantage of Jerry's confusion, Sanchez used his wind powers to fly straight up into the sky. He saw an airplane passing nearby and flew toward it with a devious plan. Meanwhile, Jerry had been cautiously waiting for a sneak attack that never came. Soon he closed his eyes and concentrated on finding Sanchez' energy aura. Jerry discovered that Sanchez was high up in the sky, so he flew up towards him and wondered, *why is he up there?*

The airplane was about to pass by Sanchez, so he closed his eyes and concentrated on the plane. This gave Jerry time to reach Sanchez and grab him, but Sanchez started laughing. Jerry squeezed him tightly and demanded, "What are you laughing at?"

"Muahahahaha! The plane you fool, look!"

The plane roared by them and suddenly veered downward! Jerry angrily interrogated Sanchez, "What have you done?"

"I told the pilot to crash into the Washington Monument! And it's all thanks to your powers! Muahahahaha!"

Jerry wanted to kill Sanchez immediately, but he knew the plane would crash within a minute or two and hundreds of people would die if Jerry did not act quickly. Jerry also needed time to figure out how to save the plane, so every second counts. Jerry reluctantly released Sanchez and flew at supersonic speed to catch up to the falling plane.

While flying towards the plane, Jerry thought about his powers and considered how to handle such a large and heavy object. Then he remembered the time he dealt with a massive building in Indonesia. However, he only held up that building temporarily and eventually made it explode, which was not an option for the airplane, but certainly gave Jerry an idea.

When Jerry finally reached the airplane, he magnetically attached himself to the top of the plane using his cyborg armor, then he began concentrating. He needed to disable the engines to slow down the plane, so he thought about ice and snow, causing freezing cold blue energy to rapidly spread from his body and envelop the entire plane! This caused the engines and controls to shut off.

However, the Washington Monument was fast approaching. It was over 500 feet tall and made of rock-hard granite and marble, strong enough to destroy the plane and kill everyone if it hits. The plane was also very heavy and traveling at about 400 mph, making it nearly impossible to maneuver. For some strange reason, Jerry randomly thought about Leah and not wanting to disappoint her, which gave him a bold idea.

As the plane was seconds away from making a direct hit, Jerry closed his eyes and manipulated the blue energy around the plane. The energy began spiking and distorting uncontrollably, like TV static or radio waves. Tourists on the ground were terrified and covered their heads, bracing for impact!

Suddenly, the plane flew right through the Washington Monument! But there was no debris, no noise, and no damage done. The plane completely phased through the monument without making contact. Tourists were relieved, but still worried as they watched the plane soar through the sky on a one-way trip to the Tidal Basin, a massive body of water.

Jerry had very little control of the plane, but he managed to use his strength and telekinetic blue energy to slightly guide the plane. He was able to slow down the plane to about 140 mph and level it out, making it somewhat parallel to the water. Soon the plane touched water and Jerry used all his remaining power to reinforce and protect the plane as it plowed through the Tidal Basin, blasting huge sprays and waves of water everywhere. The plane greatly slowed down and eventually came to a halt right in front of the Jefferson Memorial.

Nearby trees with pink flowers were blossoming, as if in celebration of the successful water landing. Everyone inside the plane was relieved and Jerry was back to his normal human form, lying on top of the plane and feeling exhausted. Emergency exits opened and passengers began to emerge, cheering and thanking Jerry for a job well done. Rescue ships soon arrived to safely evacuate everyone off the plane and onto dry land. News media vans and helicopters flooded the area to catch the scene on camera. Jerry was safe and healthy, but he had no energy to escape and was forced to answer all media questions on live television.

Leah sent mass text messages, alerting all of Jerry's family and friends about the White House battle and airplane rescue. Many people around the world enjoyed watching the footage and interview, but Detective Sanchez was furious. He watched from a secret underground bunker where the President was being held. Jerry explained Sanchez' mind control and the airplane pilot confirmed that he was unable to control himself and forced the plane to crash. TV news media and the internet were all buzzing with controversy! Most people believed Jerry, knowing he was a great hero, but some people slammed Jerry and branded him a terrorist against America. Police agreed not to arrest Jerry and provided him with a hotel room for the night so he could rest, and they watched over him as a safety precaution too.

Detective Sanchez had complete control over the President, his advisors, security, and key White House members, but he could not control the whole world and knew outside forces would come for him soon. This forced Sanchez to speed up his final plan.

Chapter 10:
BRAIN DIVE

WHILE JERRY WAS BUSY DEALING WITH ISSUES in Washington D.C., Cynthia and the Believers were having trouble with their mission.

"Excuse me officer, how are you feeling today?" Cynthia asked.

"Fine, but a bit busy at the moment, can I help you with something?"

"Yes, I was wondering if you remember being mind-controlled and attacking me a few days ago."

"Yep, that was bad, had no control of myself, sorry about that," the officer apologized.

"Are you still being mind-controlled now?"

"Nope."

"How do you know?" Cynthia inquired.

The officer impatiently answered, "Because I'm trying to do my job, numerous reporters and people have harassed me about that event, and I haven't shot them or done anything crazy yet, so I guess I'm fine. Can I get back to work now?"

Cynthia walked away feeling guilty after hearing the officer's point of view on the scenario. However, she was also annoyed that she hadn't found a single person currently being mind-controlled. Blake, Von, and Alina hadn't found anyone either. Cynthia thought of teleporting to the White House, thinking there should be people mind-controlled there, but she didn't want to interfere with Jerry's mission and wanted to complete her own mission without his help.

Feeling stumped, she asked the group what to do and Von said he wanted to visit his father's house to take care of a few things. Everyone agreed, but Cynthia couldn't teleport there because she had never visited or seen Von's house before. Luckily, Blake was able to use his NFL football connections. He made a phone call and a vehicle arrived minutes later to pick them up.

Von's home was ranch style, single-story with brown-painted walls, a black shingle roof, white window frames, and a half-circle driveway leading up to the front door. When everyone got out of the car and approached the house, they saw numerous flowers and envelopes sitting at the front door. The Believers all helped Von carry everything into his home.

The inside of Von's home almost looked like a museum. Everything was made of wood, couches and chairs were old, the dining table and other flat surfaces were dusty, the living room TV was about 35 inches with an antenna and a huge box shape in the back, and there were spiritual and religious items all around the house, including a blue-and-white dream catcher with feathers hanging above a doorway. Beyond the looks, Von's home also had a sad and neglected feeling about it. It was full of pictures and mementos of Von's parents, both of whom are dead now.

The flowers and envelopes were all gifts from people who knew Chief Grimes. The Believers offered to help open gifts and clean the house, but Von refused and told them to sit and relax for a bit. Cynthia sat down and used her phone to check in with Leah, texting her to see how she was doing. Alina sat down and watched Von, worrying about him as he opened gifts, threw away junk, cleaned the house, and made phone calls about his dead father to close out bills and affairs. After 10-15 minutes, Blake became bored and began sharing stories about his youth with Alina and Cynthia.

"My dad wasn't around much, but my mom was always on my case. She called my teachers and spoke with neighbors often to keep an eye on me. She always knew when I was causing trouble or hanging with the wrong people. She knew I wasn't great at school, so she pushed me to do chores and small jobs in the neighborhood. Whatever money I made went towards raising our family; I have a younger brother and sister. I wasn't really doing much with my life until I met Von and his parents. They let me come over to this house all the time! We had great food, video games, and a big backyard to mess around in. They taught me life lessons and helped me get better paying jobs too. All was great, until his mom died, which led to the dark times, and..."

Suddenly, everyone received a text message from Leah saying that Jerry was being interviewed on live TV. Blake grabbed the remote and turned on the TV. He checked the news stations and soon found Jerry explaining everything about the emergency plane landing and Sanchez' mind control. Everyone's eyes were glued to the TV, except for Von, who was still finishing personal matters. As Cynthia watched, she became increasingly anxious. She felt like Jerry was doing all the hero work while herself and the Believers were falling behind.

Determined to help Jerry and prove herself, Cynthia began thinking hard, trying to find a solution to her current mission. She reviewed what she already knew, thought about past events, and then an idea sparked in her mind...the importance of memories! She jumped up with excitement and discussed her idea with the Believers.

"We know it's nearly impossible to find someone who's currently mind-controlled," Cynthia declared.

"Yep," Blake acknowledged.

"And even if we did find someone, we would have to tie them down and torture them until they let us analyze their mind," Alina added.

"Damn Alina!" Blake replied with surprise.

"What?" Alina questioned.

"Isn't torture a bit dark?" Blake asked.

"So what? Sanchez is playing dirty, which means we have to as well if we expect to win," Alina retorted.

"Wow, you sound just like Von. You definitely belong with him!" Blake laughed.

Alina turned bright red and was about to answer back, but Cynthia cut her off, "You guys are missing the point. If we can't find someone who's currently mind-controlled, then we need to find someone who was mind-controlled and analyze their mind."

"How's that gonna help?" Blake wondered aloud.

"Jerry and I have used our powers in the past to analyze peoples' memories and find bad guys. What if we analyze someone's memories of being mind-controlled? That should give us answers on how to resist or negate it," Cynthia reasoned.

"Maybe, but it would have to be someone who was deeply traumatized by the experience. Someone who vividly remembers being mind-controlled and lives with the consequences. That person would have the strongest memories and give us the best information," Alina affirmed.

"Umm...have any of you looked around? I think it's obvious who we're picking," Blake pointed out and looked at Von.

Everyone else looked at Von too, and he looked back at his fellow Believers, but he wasn't thrilled. In fact, Von thought about it for a moment, Blake grinned, and then Von ran out the backdoor.

"Remember what you said about tying down and torturing someone? It's gonna happen today!" Blake exclaimed as he bolted after Von.

Alina and Cynthia immediately ran outside and watched Blake charge down Von like a lion hunting a gazelle. Being an NFL football player, Blake had an unfair advantage as he chased after Von and eventually tackled him to the ground. They began wrestling each other, rolling on the ground, and arguing back and forth.

"This is a bad idea, Blake!"

"It's the only chance we got bro!"

"You know about the dark times Blake! I can't let them see any of that!"

"You're practically dating Alina, and she's best friends with Cynthia. They were gonna find out soon anyway!" Blake retorted.

"Not like this, Blake! Not for some stupid hero mission!"

"This is the best reason to do it! Sanchez ruined your life! If this helps you fight against him, then it's worth it right?"

After Blake mentioned Sanchez, Von became furious and released a dark shockwave that blasted Blake away, sending him tumbling across the grass. Cynthia worriedly teleported next to Blake to assess him for injuries. Alina ran up to Von and yelled, "Look what this is doing to you! You're lashing out at your best friend!"

"I didn't mean to! It's just...too much...everything...it all sucks!"

"I know Von, I get it! Your mom and dad's deaths, the mind control, your suicide attempt, and all the pain you've endured is overflowing! But we can get through this together! If we analyze your mind, we'll have the power to stop Sanchez, save the world, and save you!"

Von froze as Alina's words and emotions washed over him. He looked at Blake, who was visibly hurt and upset. Then he looked at Cynthia and felt her defensiveness, she was ready to pummel Von if he even showed a hint of further aggression. But Alina was different; she wasn't scared of Von, never saw him as a threat, and truly wanted to help. She cared about him more than anyone else before.

Von dated plenty of girls in the past, but they all used him for fun and games. He was a football quarterback in high school and college, so girls viewed him as a trophy guy and wanted him for selfish reasons. They never had a deep interest in his wellbeing, but Alina did. She wanted to do everything in her power to make his life better, to help him heal and become whole again. Most importantly, she was willing to put her life and heart at stake, willing to stand by him through whatever challenges may come and ensure a brighter future for them both.

Alina read Von's mind and knew she had gotten through to him, so she decided to make her move. Wearing a short red dress with white polka dots and long, curly red hair, she confidently strutted toward Von. She tried to focus and control her power, but her emotions and desire to help Von made her aura radiate and overflow with energy, releasing flashes of red and orange light. Von watched in wonder, having never seen such beauty and power directly approach him before. Cynthia and Blake stared in awe and hoped Alina knew what she was doing.

When Alina finally reached Von, she fervently grabbed Von's shirt, pulled him in, and gave him the most passionate kiss of her life. The kiss was to distract and surprise Von, but her true intent was to perform a brain dive into Von's mind. Cynthia and Alina accidentally entered Jerry's mind in the past, but this time, Alina entered Von's mind on purpose. To everyone else, it looked like only a few seconds, but to her it felt like decades. She saw and experienced many years of Von's life, including the dark times.

***

Since Von fully trusted Alina, his mind was open to her, and she relived his life and memories. She experienced every emotion possible, starting from Von's childhood and working her way to the current time. Originally, she only planned to analyze the moment of Sanchez' mind control, but she realized that she required a deeper understanding of Von's life to analyze the full effects of Sanchez' power and how it controlled Von's mind.

As a child, Von was confident and strong, always competing against other kids for victory and fame. His friend, Blake, always followed and supported him. At home, he learned a lot from his mom, dad, and brother. His mother instilled the value of family, love, and sacrifice for the greater good. His father taught him about police duty, football, hard work, and how to be the best man possible. His brother taught him the importance of sharing and cooperation to accomplish goals.

Alina enjoyed reliving Von's life, until she came upon his mother's tragic death. She had gone grocery shopping and, on the drive back home, a male drunk driver in a pickup truck blew past a red traffic light and totaled his mom's car. She died instantly, and the perfect family unit of a wife, husband, and two kids vanished. His older brother was grief-stricken and moved out of their home. His father became a workaholic and forced Von to take over many of his mother's house duties. Von's life was forever changed, and his heart bled for years to come, leading to the dark times.

Therapy wasn't very popular when Von was a teenager, so he never learned how to properly deal with the loss of his mother. As a result, Von and Blake got into lots of trouble. Von provoked random kids and started fights at school, parties, and neighborhoods. He committed small-time crimes and misdemeanors, sometimes getting caught and bailed out of trouble thanks to his father being the police chief. He became a great football quarterback, not for fun or the love of the sport, but because he wanted to win and feel superior to everyone around him. He also liked taking big hits in football games, viewing them as punishment for not being able to save his mother's life. He even learned police work and participated in boot camps to improve his combat skills and torture himself with extreme physical training. It all culminated into one bad night where he got drunk, stole a bunch of his dead mother's belongings, and started a fire in an open field behind a church in Homestead to burn it all. Von wanted God to see and feel his pain and punish him for his sins and failures.

Alina felt a dark, gaping hole in her heart as she relived Von's worst memories. However, she also discovered a pattern. In the past, when Von trained with Jerry in his backyard, Von became angry and tried stabbing Jerry with a knife. Alina noticed something unusual at that moment; Von did not feel like he was stabbing Jerry, he felt like he was stabbing the man who killed his mother. Later, when Von shot his own father while mind-controlled, Von also felt like he was shooting the man who killed his mother.

As a result of everything above, Alina concluded that Sanchez' mind control powers work via human emotions. Everyone has emotions that guide their decision-making and overall way of living. If people are aware of being mind-controlled, they must control their own emotions, essentially forcing themselves to not feel anything. However, it is nearly impossible to do any activities without emotion because most activities and their outcomes evoke emotions out of people. Therefore, the Believers will have to train hard to learn how to control their emotions and counter Sanchez' mind control powers.

Alina mentally returned to her body, barely finished kissing Von, and fell unconscious. Von caught her in his arms and held her close, fully aware of what she'd done. She learned everything about Von and revealed all his faults and misunderstandings of the past. She also showed him the secret to countering Sanchez' mind control, which brought Von one step closer to getting revenge against him. Most importantly, she revealed her love and how far she was willing to go for him.

Knowing that he was solely responsible for Alina's exhaustion, Von picked her up and carried her into his home. Blake and Cynthia watched them pass by and wanted to speak, but felt the timing wasn't right. They did not understand what transpired, but they saw Von's stern face and felt his grim mood. They also understood that whatever happened was Alina's will, her decision, and his responsibility to bear. In silent support, Blake and Cynthia followed them back into Von's home.

Chapter 11:
CRIME & CHAOS

"THAT'S IT?" CYNTHIA ASKED.

"Yep," Von confirmed.

"All we have to do is control our emotions and we'll never be mind-controlled again?" Blake questioned.

"Yep," Von repeated.

"That's super easy!" Blake exclaimed.

"Nope," Von replied, "It's actually pretty hard."

"What do you mean? Can't I just pretend I'm a zombie or something?" Blake inquired.

"Maybe, because they're dead and can't feel anything. But they might have some emotions, like aggression when chasing people, or happiness when eating their brains," Von joked.

"Guys, I don't think you have to worry about any of that. I'm sure Alina has a plan to help you all train," Cynthia assured them.

"Yeah, if she ever wakes up," Blake blurted out. He immediately regretted his words as Von punched Blake's arm with unrelenting force. Blake ached with pain, he felt like his arm was about to fall off. Blake wanted to complain, but Von grinned, and Blake knew he deserved it.

Von, Blake, and Cynthia were sitting in the living room and reviewing everything Alina & Von learned about Sanchez' mind control. It was the next morning and they had just finished eating breakfast, about 12 hours since Alina fell unconscious. Von was worried about Alina, but he also felt relieved, like a weight had been lifted off his shoulders. He was happy to finally share his memories and hardships with Alina. His favorite part about the scenario was her drive and motivation, her taking charge to kiss him and conduct the brain dive. *Damn, that was hot!* Von thought to himself.

Blake noticed that Von was distracted, so he turned on the TV and video game system. He handed Von a control and said, "Let's play something bro, fighting game or zombie shooting, you pick."

"Zombies, I need to practice my aim for taking down Sanchez. But I'm also gonna knock out your high scores, let's do it!"

The boys began playing their games, so Cynthia walked over to visit Alina, who was lying asleep in Von's bedroom. Alina seemed comfortable and healthy, but Cynthia was still worried about her. It was Alina's first time doing a brain dive alone and she exerted all her energy.

Cynthia remembered every time Jerry overexerted himself, including when he almost died against Kevin. She also remembered overexerting herself and puking while learning how to use her powers. All the Believers struggled with their powers, but they had each other for support. Then it hit Cynthia and she realized *Jerry was the first Believer and he struggled alone for years. I met him in 10th grade, but his powers emerged as a child, and he dealt with it all on his own. Then he trained for years with the police and the FBI to become a hero and save others. Later when he met Leah and discovered her powers, it probably reminded him of his own struggles growing up, so he did everything to help her. He also helped all other Believers he met along the way.*

Cynthia's thoughts about Jerry made her smile and admire him. She valued his strength, hard work, and love for humanity. She felt herself yearning for him, as if she hadn't seen him in years. She wanted to see him again, feel his touch, and hear his voice.

Suddenly, as if Jerry could hear her thoughts, he appeared right in front of her! Anyone else would have jumped or been startled, but she was used to Jerry teleporting to her, and this time she really missed him. He was about to apologize, but Cynthia hugged him tightly for a while. Jerry felt surprised after the long hug, looked into her eyes, and said, "I missed you too." Then he kissed her on the lips and Cynthia's heart melted. She needed this moment, a break from all the chaos created by Sanchez.

After that kiss, Cynthia held Jerry's hands and asked, "What do we do with Alina? She's been unconscious for 12 hours."

"I'm assuming she's healthy or else you would have taken her to the hospital, so it should be easy to wake her up."

"How?"

"All you have to do is place your hand on Alina's head and send her waves of positive energy. Her mind should react accordingly and wake her up. Let's do it together," Jerry suggested.

He took Cynthia's hand and placed it gently on Alina's forehead, then he told her to think of something Alina really likes, something that'll energize her. Cynthia immediately thought of coffee, café con leche to be exact. She sent waves of energy simulating her feelings and memories of drinking it. Jerry also sensed Cynthia's energy and amplified her power. Afterward, Jerry smiled and motioned Cynthia to take a step back. They gave Alina some space and she quickly jolted up in bed and started rambling rapidly as if she were full of adrenaline.

"What is this? I feel amazing! I could run ten miles right now! But that would be a waste of time! Sanchez! I'm gonna kill Sanchez! I'm gonna strangle him, shoot him, and throw my shoe at him! What am I crazy? I don't have superpowers! Well, I do, but they won't hurt him. That's right! I have to train the Believers! Von! Blake! I have a plan!"

Jerry and Cynthia stared at Alina in shock, as if she was a nutcase. Alina jumped out of bed, wrapped her arms around both of them and declared, "You guys rock! Whatever you did to me worked! I feel like a whole new woman! You two should get married! I can be your Maid of Honor! But first we gotta beat Sanchez! Time to kick some ass! Von! Blake! Where are you guys?"

Alina stormed out of the bedroom and found Von and Blake sitting on a couch playing video games and completely ignoring her. They were really into, shouting commands for strategy and teamwork while killing as many zombies as possible. She uncontrollably screamed, "Are you kidding me! I just woke up from a coma and you're playing video games? Our training starts right now!"

Alina unexpectedly leapt over the couch and landed on top of Von! Blake scrambled out of the way and Von exclaimed, "What are you doing?"

"This is your training! Don't show emotions!" Alina shouted as she wrestled with Von.

Blake cheered them on and yelled, "Act like a zombie Von! You got this bro!"

Jerry & Cynthia looked at each other and laughed, knowing that all of this was 100% their fault. They only wanted to wake Alina up, but they accidentally supercharged her. This was the first time Jerry & Cynthia had ever combined their powers together, so the effects were quite unpredictable, and they wondered what else might be possible. They kept watching their friends wrestling and Cynthia asked, "Should we stop them?"

Jerry hesitated to think, but then an emergency siren began blaring from his phone! After Jerry took it out of his pocket, Leah's voice rang out and announced, "There are riots happening all over California! The U.S. President sent the National Guard to three cities in California with high crime rates, but then the people of California revolted! They claimed their rights were being violated by the National Guard and their martial law mandates. Police are trying to help, and the governor of California has declared a state of emergency! Californians are flooding social media with pictures and videos begging the Believers to come to their aid! We have to help them!"

Jerry & Cynthia instinctively held hands and proclaimed, "We got this!" Then Leah sent Jerry a text message with a video link. Jerry clicked it and saw exactly where the riots were taking place. He concentrated on the location and after a few seconds, both Jerry & Cynthia disappeared. Blake wanted to join them badly, but he knew they needed to be better prepared before taking on Sanchez, so he got pumped up and tackled both Von and Alina for training.

"Too much emotion Blake! Try to be calm and think of nothing while wrestling," Alina clarified. Her workout regimen and goals were simple: teach Von and Blake meditation and breathing techniques to eliminate emotions and thinking while fighting. If they can fight while keeping their minds calm and clear, then they can more readily defend themselves against Sanchez' mind control.

They spent all day and night training together while Jerry & Cynthia were gone.

***

When Jerry and Cynthia arrived in California, they were stunned by all the chaos happening around them. There were fallen fences and debris spread across the ground. Buildings were on fire and curse words were graffitied on the walls. Rioters were breaking windows, looting stores, and destroying property. There were people wearing masks and throwing tear gas. Protestors were fighting against police and carrying signs saying, "State Rights Matter," "Martial Law is Not Justice," "Police are Criminals," and "End Government Tyranny."

Jerry & Cynthia looked at each other and agreed that there was too much going on to work together; they needed to divide and conquer. Jerry walked up to a nearby fire hydrant, placed his hand upon it, and concentrated his power. Red energy enveloped the fire hydrant, causing the large nuts to slowly unscrew. Then water flowed out and Jerry absorbed it into and around his body! The water became thick, white, and blue, forming an armor of flowing water all over his body. Once complete, Jerry closed the fire hydrant, looked up to the sky, and blasted off like a rocket!

He flew all over the state of California, targeting wildfires and burning buildings. Anytime he saw fire, he would crash into it like a wave! He literally dove head-first into fires and his aquatic armor instantly extinguished the flames with small bursts of water. In less than an hour, Jerry put out all the fires in California, but he discovered a dangerous scenario at the end of his journey.

There were men on motorcycles driving around and they soon approached a police car with law enforcement personnel guarding it. Each motorcycle had two people on it and the backseat members were holding Molotov cocktails, fiery glass bottles capable of large explosions. Right when Jerry arrived, they all threw their Molotov cocktails at the vehicle! The officers attempted to scramble away, but they were too slow, and the police car exploded! Jerry teleported into the explosion and created a water bubble that contained and reduced the blast. The officers were knocked off their feet, but they were mostly unharmed and soon stared back in disbelief. They witnessed Jerry floating inside the water bubble for a few seconds, then he fell to the ground along with all the car debris. He was soaking wet and back to his normal form. He slowly stepped out of the debris and officers gave him thumbs-up and salutes, thanking him for saving their lives.

While Jerry dealt with his challenges, Cynthia took on plenty of her own. First, she handled the most destructive rioters in the immediate area. Many small stores were being targeted by rioters. They were using guns, bats, and other weapons to break glass windows and barge into stores to steal loot. They were destroying and ransacking everything as if it were their last day on Earth.

Cynthia initially charged into stores and tased people with her powers to knock them unconscious, as she had done previously at the capitol riot. However, she quickly realized there were far too many looters, and she needed a better plan. She thought about her powers at the molecular level and different strategies to stop the rioters. Then she had a moment of brilliance and figured out that fear could be her greatest weapon.

She closed her eyes and looked around, focusing on energy and molecules in the air. She snapped her fingers a few times and caused sparks like fireworks. She was making molecules in the air crash into each other to create the effect. Then she tested it at different ranges and concluded that it can work anywhere within her vision. She began running into stores and snapping her fingers to create fireworks and scare looters! People scattered and abandoned the stores swiftly, making Cynthia proud of herself temporarily. However, even though this method was highly effective and used less energy, it was still too slow because she needed to help multiple cities and stores more quickly.

She remembered how Jerry wrapped his own body in water, so she thought of a similar plan. She concentrated her power and absorbed air molecules into and around her body. She soon looked like an air elemental, with white and gray-colored wind flowing everywhere and making her float up into the sky. Using this new power, she was able to fly around at high speeds throughout the three major crime cities of California, blasting into stores and creating loud sonic boom noises to scare away looters. She also burst through clouds of tear gas, causing them to disperse and clear the air.

Jerry & Cynthia contacted each other and met under a tree on a secluded hilltop in California. They congratulated each other on a job well done and shared their recent stories of challenges and triumphs. They felt good about their heroic deeds and were soon ready to depart back home. However, Jerry's super hearing began picking up whispers of protestors gathering and preparing to riot again throughout California. It seemed as if Jerry & Cynthia's previous efforts were only temporarily helpful and delaying the inevitable.

Jerry crouched down in pain; he could feel peoples' resentment and desire to cause more damage and suffering. Many rioters did not care about freedom or legal rights, they used this political scenario as an excuse to commit heinous crimes. They wanted to shatter windows, destroy property, and steal from business owners for fun and to gain easy money. They took pleasure in swinging bats, shooting guns, and harming innocent people. Many of them hate police and authority, so this was the perfect chance to strike back. With so many chaotic events happening around California and authorities being overwhelmed, most of these rioters would never be found nor prosecuted.

Cynthia's ability to read Jerry's heart was vital at this moment. She felt Jerry's emotional struggle and knelt down to hug him. Jerry explained what he heard as well as what he thought would happen next, the continuation of riots in California and possibly the beginning of riots around America. Cynthia knew he felt overwhelmed, as if everyone was depending on him. She also realized that she needed to step up and do more for Jerry, the same way he helped many others over the years. Sure enough, Cynthia had an idea.

"Remember how we combined our powers to heal Alina?"

"Yeah, I was surprised it worked so well. Alina was pretty fired up," Jerry admitted.

"Well, what if we did the opposite? What if we put people to sleep?"

"Who?" Jerry asked.

"Everyone! Let's combine our powers and put all of California to sleep!"

"How?" Jerry questioned.

"My powers allow me to manipulate molecules, which means I can probably change air molecules to put people to sleep! But California is pretty big, so I need your help," Cynthia reasoned.

Jerry thought it was a crazy idea, but he had nothing else to offer and time was running out, so he agreed with her plan. Jerry sat down on the ground, closed his eyes, and deeply concentrated on his super hearing to pinpoint exactly where the largest groups of rioters were gathering. Once Jerry identified their locations, he created magical eyes above every group. Jerry used these magical eyes to see all the rioters; they had weapons, signs, and masks to invoke power and fear. They were gathering and preparing to attack businesses, police, and the National Guard. Jerry told Cynthia to prepare herself and use him as a focal point.

Cynthia followed his lead by closing her eyes and focusing her power. Her hands gradually began glowing with bright golden light. The longer she concentrated, the more it spread. Soon the light covered her entire body and shined like the sun. She placed her hands upon Jerry and began channeling her power through him. In return, Jerry projected her power through his magical eyes.

Rays of everlasting light blasted through his magical eyes and illuminated all areas with large groups of rioters in California. This light transformed the air molecules into sleep-inducing particles that affected everyone upon contact. Some rioters were scared, thinking the light came from police helicopters, and tried running away, only to fall asleep after taking a few steps. Other rioters were emboldened and tried charging to attack their enemies, but they too fell asleep seconds later. Cynthia's light momentarily grew dim as she became exhausted and drained, but Jerry noticed and quickly amplified her power, reigniting her spirit. Together, they expanded her power and successfully caused all large groups of rioters in California to fall asleep.

The police, National Guard, and the rest of California breathed a sigh of relief as the riots came to a peaceful end. Jerry & Cynthia both smiled, embraced each other, and fell asleep together under the tree upon the hilltop.

Chapter 12:
A PLAN GONE WRONG

"ARE THE NUKES READY?" SANCHEZ ASKED.

"Yes," a military advisor answered.

"Then it is time for the President of the United States to give the final order to launch," Sanchez commanded.

"Yes sir!"

The U.S. President, along with all his top military advisors, were sitting around a meeting desk in a secret underground bunker. Normally the President would have a detailed discussion with his advisors on the justification for launching nuclear weapons. During the California riots, however, Sanchez used the President to contact as many people as possible and abused his mind control powers. He enslaved an army of personnel and did everything to ensure his nuclear plan would be executed without any problems. Everyone around Sanchez served as his helpless puppets and agreed to all his requests.

The U.S. President contacted the Pentagon and pulled out a laminated card from his pocket. This card had a special challenge code that he shared with the Pentagon. Once legitimacy was confirmed, the Pentagon began preparations and informed the President that the nuclear weapons would be ready for launch in approximately 15 minutes.

Sanchez was overjoyed, feeling like his hard work had finally paid off. He was sitting in a luxurious chair drinking wine and thinking to himself.

Last year, I was a mere detective following the orders of an incompetent police chief. But now I control the President of the United States and the greatest country in the world! And to show my gratitude, I'm going to destroy it! Jerry will be on his knees begging for mercy and forced to watch his world burn to the ground! A weakling would cling to America out of fear, but with my powers, I can go anywhere, anytime, and rule as I please! The whole world is at my fingertips and ready for the taking!

Agent X, leader of the FBI, was among many other people inside the secret underground bunker. He used to work with Jerry and the Believers before being mind-controlled by Sanchez. People who are mind-controlled for long periods of time can only perform basic life functions such as eating, sleeping, or using the bathroom. They normally cannot do anything else unless ordered by Sanchez or a designated person in charge of them. However, sometimes Sanchez loses control of people when he's heavily distracted, weakened, or hasn't given someone a command in a long time...

***

As the sun rose the morning after the California riots, Jerry and Cynthia woke up together under a tree on a hilltop. They stood up feeling refreshed and stared outward. There were rolling hills, curving roads, and a vast cityscape below. Everything was quiet; no riots, exploding cars, burning buildings, nor anything crazy happening. Jerry & Cynthia held each other closely and felt relieved that California seemed to be back to normal. Soon their stomachs growled, and they needed food, but they also wanted to inform the Believers about everything that happened, so they teleported back to Von's house.

When Jerry & Cynthia arrived at Von's home, it was early morning, and everyone was asleep. They saw dirty clothes and exercise gear sprawled out everywhere, proving that the Believers trained very hard during the California riots, doing everything they could to prepare for their future battle with Sanchez. Jerry & Cynthia collected whatever food was left in the kitchen and scarfed it down. They ate buttered toast and frosted cereal with milk.

The Believers overheard breakfast sounds and gradually came out of their bedrooms. Blake walked out first, giving Jerry a thumbs up for a job well-done in California. Blake revealed that Leah had already texted the Believers about what happened, since she can maintain a constant connection to Jerry's phone and monitor the internet news feeds 24/7. Blake then prepared his own food for breakfast. Soon both Alina and Von walked out together, with messy hair and a similar hunger for food.

They all ate and shared stories about their recent activities. They smiled and enjoyed breakfast together, feeling happy and accomplished, a rare moment that hadn't occurred in months. Sanchez had caused so much pain and chaos in the past and present, but this peaceful morning gave the Believers a chance to be free of worries, to live and breathe like normal young adults. This is what Jerry wanted for the rest of his life; a safe world to live in happily ever after with friends and family. Being a superhero in constant danger was not an option anymore. Maybe after defeating Sanchez, Jerry could use his powers for humanitarian efforts and make the world a better place for Leah and all children of the future.

Unfortunately, their breakfast came to an abrupt end when Jerry received an unexpected and troubling message from Agent X.

"Jerry! Come quickly and bring the Believers! Sanchez, the U.S. President, and his top advisors set actions in motion to launch nuclear weapons! But maybe if you stop Sanchez and restore the President's mind, he can call off the nuclear launch! We are all here in a secret underground bunker. But be careful, Sanchez' mind control powers are strong, and he's got an army protecting the area. I'll send you the coordinates now."

Agent X sent a follow-up message with coordinates and a map of the surrounding area. Jerry read everything aloud and the Believers began preparing themselves. Von gathered bulletproof police gear and guns for himself and Blake. Jerry and Cynthia quickly hatched a plan to access the secret underground bunker. Alina wanted to join, but she still did not have combat experience, despite all her training, and did not want to be a burden in the fight. However, Alina opened her phone and began reviewing contacts to see if anyone else could help. When the Believers finalized preparations, Alina kissed Von goodbye, then Jerry concentrated on the bunker location, held hands with Cynthia, Blake, and Von, and they all disappeared in a flash.

The Believers reappeared in a grassy field in the middle of nowhere. There were no buildings or any signs of civilization. However, there were soldiers standing around in different spots. They noticed the Believers and pointed their guns at them, but Jerry swiftly created a blue forcefield around himself and the Believers. Bullets began raining down and bouncing off the forcefield.

Cynthia remembered her part of the plan, sat on the ground, and began concentrating. She sent waves of energy into the ground and soon discovered the exact location of the secret underground bunker; it was a few meters away from where the Believers stood. Cynthia used her powers to transform the molecules of the ground above the bunker! The ground molecules moved underneath the bunker and forced the bunker upward like a volcano! When the bunker rose to the surface, it was like a steel box the size of a house.

At this point, there were over a hundred soldiers, many wearing camouflage to blend in with the grass. Thousands of bullets had been fired and blocked by Jerry's forcefield. Jerry changed the color of his forcefield from blue to red and blasted it outward, sending all the bullets back at the soldiers. About half the soldiers took direct hits and fell down, groaning in pain but still alive, while the other soldiers stopped firing their guns and dove to the ground for safety. This gave Von and Blake their chance to attack.

Thanks to many previous training sessions, they utilized their powers in newfound ways. Blake roared and powered up, doubling his size and police gear to look like a tank! Then he charged at half the soldiers and barreled through them! He sent them flying in all directions like bowling pins! Von pulled out an assault rifle and charged at the other half of soldiers, firing his gun and taking down as many enemies as possible. When they fired back at Von, he took a few hits to his bulletproof armor, but he dodged most bullets at high speed and never slowed down. The green grass also changed to dead black anywhere Von stepped, as if he were sucking the life energy out of the ground to strengthen himself. Most of the soldiers did not die thanks to their protective gear, but they were severely injured or unconscious.

Cynthia was still on the ground, taking a moment to rest after expending power to bring the underground bunker up to the surface. Jerry confidently approached the bunker and a door opened. Several more armed personnel charged out of the bunker and began taser guns. Jerry created a blue force wall that stopped the tasers and absorbed the electricity, then he changed the forcefield from blue to red and fired bolts of electricity at all his enemies! They were all electrocuted and fell unconscious.

The moment Jerry's forcefield disappeared, Sanchez shot out of the bunker like a rocket! He used tornado winds to propel himself at full speed into Jerry, who was caught by surprise and unable to dodge. Sanchez had a powerful wind attack charged up in his fist and punched Jerry at full power, knocking him over a hundred feet away! Jerry's body flew past Cynthia and tumbled violently across the ground.

Feeling victorious, Sanchez let out a mocking laugh and felt 100% confident that he could easily defeat Jerry again. Cynthia, however, was furious and suddenly grappled Sanchez with molecular webbing! He treated it as a joke and tried teleporting out of it, but he was immediately electrocuted by the webbing, and it disrupted his teleportation! She angrily swung him around like a laundry bag and slammed him into the ground! Sanchez created wind around his body to soften the hit, but he still got hurt and couldn't believe Cynthia's power.

While Sanchez was recovering on the ground, Cynthia did not let up. She charged and kicked Sanchez with a burst of wind that sent him flying toward Jerry! Jerry was now fully recovered, so he caught Sanchez and bear-hugged him tightly so he couldn't escape. Surprisingly, Sanchez did not struggle, he just smiled as if he'd already won.

Jerry shouted at Cynthia to go find the U.S. President, so she transformed herself into an air elemental and flew into the bunker looking for him. Jerry continued holding Sanchez and used his super hearing to listen to Cynthia inside. She stormed through the bunker, blasting past most guards and knocking out anyone who got in her way. After a minute or two, she found the U.S. President and teleported with him back outside next to Jerry and Sanchez. The U.S. President was alive, but non-responsive and stood there like a zombie. Jerry squeezed Sanchez tighter and commanded him to release his mind-control.

Sanchez laughed and replied, "Sure, you can have him back, but it's not going to help you." Sanchez snapped his fingers and the U.S. President's mind slowly returned to normal, as if he was coming out of a daze.

"Mr. President! Please stop the nuclear launch!" Cynthia pleaded.

"Huh, oh, yes! I'll make the call right now!" He affirmed and took out his cellphone, then he called the Pentagon and got into a heated argument! It was too late to cancel the nuclear launch! The U.S. President continued making phone calls, desperately trying to prevent a nuclear war, and Jerry began interrogating Sanchez.

"Where are the nukes being launched from?"

"I have no idea! Nobody does!" Sanchez answered in a joking manner.

"Where are the nukes going?"

"To Russia! I'm going to wipe out our greatest enemy! And if we're lucky, they'll destroy us too! Muahahahahaha!" Sanchez laughed maniacally.

"Why are you doing this? What's the point?" Jerry demanded.

"America is hopeless! Full of crime and insubordination! Citizens are constantly killing each other with guns, drugs, and alcohol! I worked as a cop and detective for years, but it changed nothing! Then I controlled the President and tried stopping crime with martial law, but everyone revolted! All my efforts failed because America is ungovernable! As for Russia, their President is untrustworthy due to his recent declaration of wanting to launch nukes against Ukraine. He also hates America and will use any excuse to fire nukes back at us. Once Russia and America destroy each other, I can use my mind control power to enslave China and rule the world!"

Cynthia unforgivingly slapped Sanchez across the face. She hit him so hard that his head turned, and his brown cheek bruised into a light red color. He took it well, almost too well, as he smiled with a devious grin. This made Cynthia angry, as if her strength meant nothing to him. She motioned to slap him again but was interrupted by Agent X running out of the bunker with his phone in hand and announcing, "The nukes just launched from Wyoming! You have to stop them before they reach orbit!"

Jerry was anxious and worried about the nukes, but Cynthia was enraged and wanted to kill Sanchez. Jerry felt her emotions and feared that her anger would lead to mistakes or collateral damage, so he told Cynthia, "Go take care of the nukes! I'll hold Sanchez here!"

Cynthia wanted to argue, but she knew there wasn't enough time, so she turned toward the state of Wyoming and blasted off! In her air elemental form, she literally becomes the wind and can travel at incredibly high speeds. She did not need to fly all the way there, only close enough to see the nuclear missiles, then she can teleport ahead of them and stop them...somehow.

After Cynthia left, more soldiers arrived to fight the Believers, including helicopters! The helicopters fired missiles at Jerry and his surrounding area, putting Agent X and the U.S. President in danger! Sanchez grinned, "What are you gonna do Jerry? Hold me tight or watch everyone die?"

With only seconds to spare, Jerry unwillingly let Sanchez go and created a blue forcefield to protect everyone around him. Now that Sanchez was free, he instantly teleported out of the way just before the missiles exploded against the forcefield. The impact of missiles created a smokescreen that blinded and distracted Jerry, giving Sanchez an advantage.

Instead of trying to attack Jerry, Sanchez teleported near Blake and Von and tried using his mind control powers against them! They were fighting soldiers and caught by surprise. They momentarily experienced mental pain like a migraine, but they recognized this sensation since they had been mind-controlled in the past. Von and Blake remembered their training and shut down all their emotions. They successfully thwarted the mind-control, but not without consequences. The mind control was a continuous effect, requiring Von and Blake to constantly resist it, which cost them plenty of mental energy. As a result, they were only able to defend themselves or hide. They couldn't attack their enemies because it was too difficult to focus, and it would invoke aggressive emotions which may cause them to be mind-controlled. They were no longer able to help...Jerry would have to finish the fight alone.

During the smokescreen, Jerry safely moved Agent X and the U.S. President into the bunker. Jerry also transformed himself; he was now covered head-to-toe in thick gray metal armor. When he exited the bunker, the helicopters spotted him and fired machine guns, but all the bullets harmlessly bounced off his armor. Jerry responded by launching himself into a helicopter propellor! He crashed right through the helicopter blades, using his armor like a wrecking ball to destroy the propellor. The helicopter made an emergency landing and smashed into the ground. The soldiers were not dead, but certainly out of commission for the rest of the battle.

Jerry made quick work of all the remaining helicopters by using the same strategy. Soon the grassy fields were littered with scrap metal and debris from the battle. Sanchez was enraged and couldn't believe his army failed to kill Jerry and his friends. He summoned all his remaining power and created a massive tornado! All the metal debris and injured soldiers were swept up into the tornado, including Von and Blake!

Jerry was heavy and well-grounded thanks to his metal armor, but that's exactly what Sanchez hoped for. Sanchez used the tornado like a cannon and began firing everything directly at Jerry! Scrap metal, debris, and helpless humans were being hurled at Jerry like projectiles! Jerry put his metal arms up and defended himself, but he knew the soldiers and his friends would die if he didn't act quickly.

The tornado created a smokescreen and Jerry guessed that Sanchez' vision may be hindered. Therefore, Jerry calmed his mind and used his powers to locate Sanchez' energy aura and exact location. Sanchez' aura was red and black, fueled by rage and pure evil, so he was easy to find. Then Jerry focused on the energy aura and teleported right behind Sanchez! He swiftly grabbed Sanchez' head and unleashed intense electrical energy, frying his brain and causing his body to fall limp onto the ground. Sanchez was unable to think or move, but his eyes were open, and he was barely conscious.

The tornado ended and everything and everyone caught in it fell to the ground. Most of the soldiers survived, including Von and Blake. Jerry transformed back into his normal human form, but he kept his hands on Sanchez' head and began concentrating his power. He wanted to try something new, something he'd never done before, and thought to himself.

For years I've given people powers by mistake, but eventually I managed to give Cynthia my powers on purpose. Her success and heroic use of my powers proved that it was not a mistake. It also proved that I could control who receives my powers and to what degree. Cynthia's powers are far greater than anyone else because I love and trust her to use them wisely. Therefore, I should be able to take away someone's powers if needed. I don't want to kill Sanchez like I did with Kevin, so I hope this works.

Jerry prayed to God, asking for Sanchez' powers to be released and absorbed back into himself. Jerry also apologized, feeling like every evil act Sanchez committed was his own fault due to accidentally giving Sanchez powers. Jerry relaxed and began absorbing Sanchez' powers, but he also received horrible memories and flashbacks of every terrible thing Sanchez had ever done with his powers. Sanchez killed many people and forced others to commit heinous crimes to further his goals. Jerry endured unbearable pain, knowing that Sanchez' memories would forever haunt him, but he bravely finished the process and completely drained Sanchez of all his powers.

Sanchez was unable to think or move, but he was awake throughout the process. He watched and sensed his powers being drained. He felt dread, torture, and then emptiness, as if everything he cared about was stripped away. When Jerry finished, Sanchez was still unable to speak or act. Then Jerry received an emergency message from Leah explaining that Cynthia needed help. Jerry immediately teleported away, and Sanchez was lying on the ground alone.

Sanchez had nothing left to live for, all he wanted was revenge, nothing else mattered now. He allowed his hate to overflow and silently pleaded to the powers of evil for help. His mind, heart, body, and soul were all focused on revenge, and he was willing to give up everything for it. Such thoughts can be dangerous and drive a man insane. Sanchez felt himself falling into a mental abyss, until he heard a voice in his head that wasn't his own.

Chapter 13:
DEATH TO ALL

"Hey Cynthia, can you do me a quick favor?"

"Sure, Jerry. What do you need?"

"I'd like you to save the world from nuking itself."

"That's it? Sounds pretty easy. Do you want me to pick up dinner on the way home too?"

"That would be great! Thanks babe, you're the best."

Cynthia was sarcastically talking to herself, complaining about Jerry sending her on an insane mission to stop nuclear bombs currently in flight. She wondered why Jerry did not go himself, thinking that he had more experience as a superhero. However, she also remembered that he willingly shared his powers with her, so hypothetically, she's just as powerful as Jerry and can do whatever he can do, so long as she believes in herself. She also just finished a short phone call with Dr. Wang explaining how to stop the nukes. She felt slightly more confident as she flew closer to the nuclear launch site in Wyoming.

Eventually she arrived and saw ten nuclear missiles high up in the sky; they were only a few minutes away from orbit and she had to stop all of them. She took a deep breath, stared at the missiles, and teleported a few miles above them. It was anxiety-inducing to see missiles flying toward her at thousands of miles per hour.

With only seconds to act, she extended her arms and hands outward and used her power to manipulate the molecules in the air, condensing them together tightly enough to form an impenetrable wall around herself and across the sky. Then she braced for impact and the missiles crashed into her wall! The missiles exploded and both fire and smoke shot out everywhere.

When the smoke cleared, Cynthia wiped sweat off her forehead and couldn't believe her strategy worked. She was worried about the exploding missiles, but they were not nuclear yet. Dr. Wang previously clarified that the nuclear fission process occurs after the missiles reach orbit, which is why Agent X told Cynthia to stop the missiles beforehand.

After taking a moment to breathe, however, Cynthia noticed a significant decline in her energy levels. She was having trouble maintaining her air elemental form and flight in the sky. Defending against those nuclear missiles really took it out of her. Thankfully the mission was complete, and she could rest for a while, or so she thought. She received a frantic phone call from Agent X claiming that Russia just launched nuclear missiles against America in retaliation!

Cynthia ended the phone call and slightly panicked internally. She now realized the extreme pressures of being a superhero. She could easily teleport to another country and rest, hoping that America successfully defends itself with technology against the nuclear attack. Or she could be a superhero and risk her life again to save America. She knew that her current energy levels were too low to fight the threat and she would have to use her own life force, like Jerry had done multiple times in the past. However, Jerry was always on the ground and fell unconscious with the chance that others could save him. Cynthia, unfortunately, would be high up in the sky, falling to her death, with very little time or hope for anyone to save her. She concluded that this was a suicide mission. Wanting more information and options, Cynthia called Dr. Wang.

"Dr. Wang, are you there? I have to ask you something."

"Sure Cynthia, honestly I'm surprised you're still alive and I hope you're heading home to rest."

"I wish I could, but Russia launched nukes back at us and I have to stop them before it's too late!"

"Cynthia, you're lucky you survived. I'm assuming you used up most of your energy and you're calling me because you don't think you can stop the Russian nukes. You're hoping I have an easier solution, but I don't."

"Dr. Wang, please help, you have to think of something! Millions of lives are at stake!"

"Jeez, you sound just like Jerry. But sometimes you must accept your limits. I'm glad you did not die, and I thank you for trying your best, but you are a good person and don't deserve to die. Please save yourself."

"No, Jerry is different! He would have sacrificed himself without hesitation. I'm not as heroic as Jerry and I thought of running away, but I couldn't live with myself knowing that everyone died because I didn't try. There must be another way, please help!" Cynthia begged.

Dr. Wang shook her head in silence, knowing that Cynthia would never accept *No* for an answer, so she took a moment to think. She knew Cynthia made a wall to stop the original nukes, which required immense energy to absorb the impact and explosions, so now she needed an indirect approach that required less energy. Then it hit her...instead of stopping the nukes, why not slow them down? Dr. Wang explained her theory to Cynthia, then she ended the phone call and hoped for the best.

Cynthia sent a message to Agent X promising that she would slow down the nuclear missiles, but America would have to shoot them down. Agent X responded with the coordinates and a distant picture of the Russian nuclear launch site. Then Cynthia read the coordinates, concentrated on the picture, and teleported there.

Cynthia was now floating above the Russian nuclear launch site. It was cold and snowy conditions, something Cynthia was not prepared for. She shivered as she looked up and saw multiple nuclear missiles parting clouds and streaking upward. She thought of her powers and Dr. Wang's advice, then she teleported several miles up into the sky. Once again, she saw a dozen nuclear missiles flying toward her and wondered about her chance of survival. She mumbled a sorrowful farewell to Jerry, then tapped into her life force, spread her arms out wide, and screamed at the top of her lungs.

"RAAAAAAAAAAAAHH!!!"

The sky all around and above Cynthia instantly transformed into numerous layers of ice all connected by molecular webbing! It was like a whole new atmosphere had been added to the earth, but only located where the missiles had to travel. Cynthia expended all her remaining energy and blacked out. Her body fell downward, and the missiles soared past her, then they hit severe turbulence. The missiles struggled to push through as the ice was building up and sticking to them.

This ice phenomenon slowed down the missiles and gave America just enough time to launch countermeasures, successfully shooting down all the nuclear missiles. Explosions lit up the sky like fireworks, as if the earth were celebrating its victory against Sanchez and the nuclear war. Cynthia, however, continued falling to her death, her unconscious body streaming down through clouds and snow at about 130 mph.

It was at this moment that Leah sent an emergency message to Jerry telling him to help Cynthia. Jerry had just finished draining Sanchez of all his powers. Since Jerry & Cynthia are always connected by their hearts and shared energy, Jerry easily figured out her exact location and teleported to her. He appeared in mid-air next to her, grabbed her, fell with her for a few seconds, and then teleported with her to a safe place...his parents' house.

***

At the Millers' home, Mr. and Mrs. Miller were hosting multiple guests: Alina, Mega Fist, Mr. Cream, and Johnny Bear. Alina was sharing everything she knew about Sanchez and the Believers' involvement in the California riots and recent nuclear attack. Mega Fist was listening and massaging his enlarged hands. He wanted revenge against Sanchez for putting him in the hospital; he stayed there for a while due to a head injury he received during a previous battle where Sanchez mind-controlled him to fight the Believers. Mr. Cream enjoyed using his powers to make ice cream for everyone, but he wanted to shut down Sanchez for moral reasons; he felt like having superpowers was a miracle and something to cherish, but Sanchez squandered it, and Mr. Cream hated him for it. Mr. Cream was so determined that he even went back to the police station with Mr. Miller, and they convinced Johnny Bear to help.

Mr. and Mrs. Miller listened carefully and absorbed the information provided, but they also admired Jerry's friends coming together for a righteous cause. Mr. Miller wanted to fight alongside them, but he loved his wife and knew that protecting her would put Jerry's mind at ease and allow him to fight without worries. Mrs. Miller was proud of everyone and tried to provide the best hospitality for them as they prepared for battle.

Once Alina finished talking, Johnny Bear heroically stood up and gave a speech, "Alright guys, clearly we are the B team, the best team! Jerry and his pals were too scared to bring us along because we'd steal the show and beatdown the bad guys too quickly!"

"Yeah, I'm sure the threat of being mind-controlled had nothing to do with Jerry's decision," Alina remarked sarcastically.

"Hey! No interruptions from the peanut gallery! I got this! Now here's the plan, Alina will approach Sanchez and seduce him! While he's distracted, Mr. Cream will freeze him! Then Mega Fist and I will finish the job; we'll bash Sanchez into crushed ice and the whole world will be saved!"

"I'm not seducing Sanchez; I have a boyfriend!" Alina retorted.

"Don't worry about your boyfriend, he'll understand, you gotta save the world, right? If ya need help, you can practice with me bebe."

"Eww, gross!" Alina expressed her disgust at the idea and everyone else laughed and agreed with her. Johnny Bear was slightly disappointed that his plan was rejected, but he was ready to come up with another one. Before Bear could speak again, however, Jerry and Cynthia suddenly appeared in the middle of the living room! Everyone was surprised and immediately concerned when they saw Cynthia unconscious. Mrs. Miller went to the kitchen to gather food and water for her. Mr. Miller went to the master bedroom and bathroom to get medicine and a blanket for her. Alina began using her powers to read Cynthia's mind and assess her health while Jerry laid her on the couch to rest.

"What happened?" Mr. Cream asked with a worried tone.

"Fighting Sanchez triggered a nuclear war and Cynthia stopped it all," Jerry answered.

Alina finished reading Cynthia's mind and angrily shouted at Jerry, "Did you send her to stop freaking nukes? Why didn't you go?"

"I was busy with Sanchez and Cynthia was the best choice."

"You were more experienced! You could've handled the nukes better than her!" Alina snapped.

"Cynthia was going to kill Sanchez! I couldn't let that happen; it would haunt her for the rest of her life. She also has a science and medical background, so I trusted her to handle the nukes on a molecular level if needed," Jerry explained.

Alina was about to continue arguing, but Johnny Bear cut her off, "This is a win! You beat Sanchez, she stopped the nukes, and everyone survived! We should celebrate!"

Mega Fist, sitting calmly in the corner of the room, chimed into the conversation, "Where are Von and Blake? We sparred against each other months ago and they owe me a rematch."

Jerry was about to reply, but Leah's voice blared out of Jerry's cellphone, "Something terrible is happening back at the President's bunker! Sanchez has new powers and both Von and Blake are fighting alone against an army of monsters! You have to help them! Bring everyone!"

"That's impossible! I drained all of Sanchez' powers!" Jerry distraughtly responded.

"Maybe you shoulda let Cynthia kill him after all," Alina snidely remarked.

Feeling guilty, but determined to right the wrong, Jerry declared, "We don't have time to argue, let's help Von and Blake end this once and for all! Believers unite!"

Alina, Mega Fist, Johnny Bear, Mr. Cream, and Mr. Miller gathered around Jerry and Mrs. Miller was greatly surprised. Mr. Miller looked at his wife and said, "I need to help our son and these kids. They are the future. Please understand...I love you."

Mrs. Miller supported him and replied, "Do your best and I'll take care of Cynthia."

Mr. Miller nodded, then Jerry concentrated for a moment and the Believers disappeared.

Chapter 14:
SANCHEZ, THE UNDYING

"SANCHEZ...I HEAR YOU..."

"Who are you?" Sanchez asked.

"Dark...ness..."

"Can you help me? I'll give anything!" Sanchez begged.

"Sacrifice...everything?"

"Yes, but only if it's worth it. I need enough power to kill Jerry and destroy the world!"

"You will have it...for your soul..."

"Yes! Take it! Grant me ultimate power and I'll kill everyone!"

"As...you...wish..."

This entire conversation was happening inside Sanchez' mind while Jerry was gone. Sanchez was lying on the floor and seemingly unconscious. Nobody was mind-controlled anymore, everyone was able to act freely. However, several men were injured from fighting against the Believers. There were hundreds of soldiers and government personnel making phone calls, reporting to their superiors, and helping the injured. Agent X, the U.S. President, and his advisors were evacuated first while everyone else had to wait for emergency services and vehicles to arrive.

Von and Blake were resting after the intense battle. Blake sat on the ground next to Von and talked about finally going back to a normal life playing football in the NFL. He enjoyed being a superhero, but only temporarily. He had gotten used to having money and fame as a football player. He also supported his entire family now, so risking his life as a superhero no longer made sense. He had a lot to live for, so he stood up slowly, stretched his back, and told Von they should leave.

Von, however, was contemplating what to do about Sanchez. He wanted to kill Sanchez for everything he'd done to his family and friends. He wasn't afraid to kill him because he felt it was justified. Von had also killed bad guys as a cop, always while saving the innocent and preventing more deaths. Nevertheless, Von hesitated after hearing Blake's story. It made him think about building a future with Alina, starting a family, and living happily ever after. He might even ask for a desk job or training job as a promotion; should be easy to get after saving the world and it would be a safer profession in the long run. He concluded that killing Sanchez would not help his future goals, nor bring his parents back to life.

Blake extended a strong hand to Von and helped him up onto his feet. Von took one last look at Sanchez, who was now surrounded by soldiers. They were preparing to arrest Sanchez and take him away. However, Von felt something strange; dark energy and wild brainwaves emitting from Sanchez! Von shouted a warning at the soldiers, but they did not understand, and they hesitated, then Sanchez screeched in pain and released a burst of negative energy! His own clothes and skin disintegrated instantly! Black smoke quickly spread from Sanchez into the surrounding area; screams could be heard from all soldiers as the smoke enveloped them.

Blake and Von saw the smoke rushing toward them and put their arms up in defense. Soon the smoke cleared and revealed a horrific scene. Sanchez, along with hundreds of soldiers and government personnel, were no longer human...they were undead. Sanchez was all bones with a menacing aura of pure evil. Everyone else was now turned into zombies with rotting flesh. Blake and Von were the only ones unaffected...everyone else was lost. Blake's aura of Believer energy instinctually protected him from the smoke's effects, but Von's energy did not react at all. As the smoke washed over Von, he felt completely unaffected and immune to it.

Blake and Von were now surrounded by zombies and the battle for their life began. Blake angrily charged through hordes of zombies like a bulldozer, trying to reach Sanchez, but there were too many and they stacked up like a cluttered wall of corpses that stopped Blake just a few feet before the villain. Sanchez then screamed at the corpses, empowering them, and causing them to overpower Blake and topple over him!

Von was also fighting zombies, but he was having lots of trouble. Since they were mindless, he could not read their thoughts to gain any advantage in combat. His bullets were also less effective, only harming the undead if he shot their heads. With so many zombies attacking Von at once, it was also difficult to shoot his guns accurately...he was inevitably overwhelmed.

In a timely fashion, Jerry, Alina, Mega Fist, Johnny Bear, Mr. Cream, and Mr. Miller arrived to help! They teleported right into the thick of it and started fighting immediately. Mr. Miller, Mega Fist, and Johnny Bear began clobbering their way through zombies with their fists and bear claws. Mr. Cream blasted waves of cold energy at zombies, causing them to freeze in place. Alina focused her mind and located both Von and Blake under a pile of zombies, then she rushed towards them with the Believers. Jerry transformed into his classic cyborg armor and began bashing his way through zombies, knocking them away like ragdolls as he made his way towards Sanchez.

When Jerry finally reached Sanchez, however, he felt something sinister and familiar. Sanchez was radiating with powerful negative energy, the same as the darkness that attacked the sun when Jerry was in outer space. Sanchez was also no longer himself...he was a monstrous skeleton with black smoke constantly fuming out of his corpse. Nonetheless, Jerry foolishly called out to the creature, trying to reach its non-existing humanity.

"Sanchez! You have to stop this now!"

"Cower in fear!" The monster roared and released another cloud of black smoke across the battlefield!

Most of the Believers cried out in pain, completely paralyzed by fear, and struggling to breathe! Jerry could no longer see his friends nor enemies, so he thought of creating wind to get rid of the smoke. Unfortunately, the monster expected this and sucker-punched Jerry with a giant fist of dark energy, sending him tumbling across the ground! Several nearby zombies jumped onto him and began clawing and biting his cyborg armor. He defended himself while drowning in regret, realizing that he should have blasted the monster into oblivion when he had the chance.

***

Alina and the Believers freed Von just before the black smoke spread and Von instinctively hugged Alina to protect her. While everyone else was paralyzed by the smoke, Von was inexplicably immune to its effects and his energy safeguarded Alina too. Von could not see his friends, but he could hear their cries of pain and was scared to let go of Alina, so he took out his police cuffs and handcuffed his left wrist to Alina! Von's energy now flowed through the handcuffs and protected Alina from the effects of the black smoke.

Alina thanked Von and then she closed her eyes. She used her powers to find the minds of all the Believers within the smoke. She sensed that their minds were filled with immense fear that paralyzed them, so they were barely able to breathe and defend themselves from danger. She quickly explained the situation to Von.

"Von! The Believers are in danger! We need to find and protect them at all costs! I'll use my powers to guide you through the smoke. Kill anything that gets in your way, they're all zombies and no longer human."

Von agreed and followed orders, but it was easier said than done. Since Von and Alina were handcuffed together, Von could only fight with his legs and one arm. They slowly moved through the smoke, fighting through zombies to reach the Believers.

They first found Mr. Cream, who was frozen in his own dome of ice. A large group of zombies were pounding on the dome, trying to break inside. Von fought off the zombies one by one using a combination of physical attacks and gunshots. Alina analyzed the scene and decided, "I think he's safer inside the ice, he must have frozen himself as a self-defense mechanism. We should help the other Believers first and come back here later."

Von agreed and they continued fighting their way through smoke and zombies to the next Believers. They soon found both Mega Fist and Johnny Bear lying on the ground, covering their head and body with their enlarged fists and claws, whining in fear as numerous zombies were attacking them. Alina knew that Von could not fight all the zombies while handcuffed to her, so she begged Von to let her go.

"Von! There's too many of them, you need both hands to fight! Give me the key!"

"No! I won't put you in danger!"

"You have to Von, please! I'm a Believer too! I knew what I was getting myself into when I joined the team and I think I can defend myself against the effects of the smoke."

"How?" Von questioned.

"Jerry was immune to Sanchez' mind control and the black smoke because his power was the original source and stronger than our powers, which we received by accident. Cynthia has powers and immunities similar to Jerry because he chose to share his powers with her, voluntarily designating her as an equal source of power. You are immune to the black smoke because your powers changed after you were mind-controlled. Your powers became darker, related to death, as a self-defense mechanism to keep you alive in the Colorado snow forest and help you cope with accidentally killing your father. With all this knowledge, I might be able to modify my own powers and protect myself against the black smoke. If it works, I may even be able to save everyone else, but I won't know until I try!"

Von hesitated, but he knew Mega Fist and Johnny Bear were hurting. They were already bleeding from multiple bites and cuts and were still being attacked by zombies. Von unwillingly gave Alina the key and she uncuffed herself. She covered her mouth and nose, crouched down, and concentrated her powers, trying to counteract the effects of the black smoke.

Von angrily dove onto the undead, losing control as he viciously attacked everything in sight. He felt himself giving into the darkness, absorbing the black smoke and allowing it to fuel his rage. He grew in speed and strength, punching holes through zombies' bodies, smashing heads together, and efficiently killing everything around his friends.

When all the enemies were vanquished, Von looked back at Alina. She was enveloped in clear white energy. She was struggling to keep the black smoke effects at bay. Then she touched both Mega

Fist and Johnny Bear, covering them in her energy as well. Their fear disappeared and they returned to normal. They were able to speak, think, and defend themselves once again, but they were visibly injured and weakened.

Alina smiled, knowing that her training had paid off. However, she noticed a change in Von's appearance. His eyes were now pitch black and his energy was cold and dark. He was in the zone, 100% focused on the battle and nothing else. He stared at Alina, speechless and waiting for orders. Alina swiftly realized what he wanted, so she pointed in a direction and said, "Blake and Mr. Miller are over there!" Von charged into the smoke and disappeared. Alina, Mega Fist, and Johnny Bear stayed together and followed slowly behind.

Von was now on his own, just the way he liked it. He completely let loose and demolished everything in his path. He elbowed a zombie so hard that it crashed through other zombies and knocked them down like bowling pins. He swept his leg under a zombie to trip it, then he grabbed its foot and swung it like a hammer multiple times, smashing several other zombies into the ground. Wanting to reach Blake faster, he grabbed a broken helicopter door and used it as a battering ram to charge through hordes of zombies. Negative energy flowed in and around Von as he continued increasing in power. This energy would drive most people mad as it did Sanchez, but Von's previous experiences and training allowed him to maintain his sanity.

Soon he came upon a large pile of zombies about ten feet high and heard Blake, his best friend, groaning in pain at the bottom. Von knew he didn't have time to fight them all one-by-one, so he desperately tried something new. He had already absorbed lots of dark energy, so he thrusted both his hands deep into the pile and released it all at once! An explosion of negative energy blasted apart most of the zombies, causing body parts to scatter everywhere.

There were only two zombies left, lying on top of Blake, and gnawing his body. Von ripped them off Blake and tossed them aside like trash, then he knelt down and checked his condition. Blake was bleeding profusely, suffering from multiple bite wounds. It was a miracle he survived so long, but Blake was unconscious and had little time left...he was going to die. Von only knew one person who could save Blake, so he looked up to the sky and screamed, "JEEEEERRRRRRRYY!!!!!!"

***

While the Believers struggled to survive in the black smoke, Jerry fought against Sanchez and his zombie army. In his monstrous skeletal form, empowered with negative energy, Sanchez was able to instantly appear anywhere inside the black smoke to bully Jerry. Sanchez blasted dark energy at Jerry, waited for him to block it, then appeared next to him and kicked him into hordes of zombies! Jerry recovered and destroyed zombies with his cyborg arms and super strength, beating zombies like piñatas and smashing them into piles of bones. However, the bones would slowly rebuild themselves into functional zombies and continue fighting. Sometimes new zombies rose out of the ground too!

Sanchez continued finding new ways to annoy Jerry and he even disintegrated his cyborg armor! During battle, Sanchez grabbed Jerry and imbued dark energy into his cyborg armor, causing it to completely corrode and fall off his body. At this point, Jerry's anger peaked, and he transformed into a demonic dragon! He had black draconic wings, enlarged muscles, pulsating veins, demonic claws, a thorned tail, and electricity crackling around his body.

Despite Jerry's transformation, Sanchez appeared unfazed. As a skeletal monster filled with dark energy, discerning his emotions was almost impossible. However, Sanchez demonstrated conscious thought and stood still, waiting for Jerry to attack.

Jerry charged full speed at Sanchez and thrust a demonic claw right through his chest! Jerry thought this was a killing blow, but Sanchez swiftly grabbed Jerry's arm, then his bones multiplied several times and wrapped around Jerry's body! Sanchez proceeded to slam Jerry repeatedly into the ground and he grunted in pain with each hit. Jerry eventually roared and unleashed a shockwave of electrical energy that tased Sanchez and freed himself. Then he swung around and whipped Sanchez with his thorned tail, causing bones to break off his body. Wanting to end the battle, Jerry blasted a massive cone of fire out of his mouth that completely engulfed Sanchez and everything around him!

Jerry wasn't sure if he killed Sanchez and couldn't see him through the black smoke, but he heard a familiar voice calling out from nearby...it was his father. Mr. Miller was a bit tired, but not paralyzed because he protected himself with a barrier of red energy. Jerry transformed back to normal and rushed over to his father. Mr. Miller smiled, feeling glad that his son was alive and well.

"Son, I saw you fighting out there...you did great...ugh..."

"Dad! Are you okay?"

"Yeah...I'm alright...just need Cuban coffee and a good night's sleep," Mr. Miller joked.

Jerry was worried about his father, so he put his arm around him and gave him a little bit of his own energy. Mr. Miller brightened up and thanked his son for the boost, then he suggested they go looking for the other Believers, noting that they may need healing and help too. Just as they were ready to leave, Sanchez leaped out of the smoke and tried attacking Jerry! Mr. Miller, however, was refreshed and alert, so he instinctively grabbed and wrapped his arms around Sanchez to protect his son!

At that exact moment, Jerry heard Von screaming his name and Mr. Miller commanded his son to go help his friends. Jerry tried to argue, but Mr. Miller began squeezing Sanchez like a vice grip and yelled, "Go now!" Mr. Miller created red energy that enveloped Sanchez' entire body. He screeched and emitted powerful waves of dark energy, but he seemed unable to escape...for now. Jerry trusted his father and knew his friends were in danger, so he rushed towards Von's voice, hoping that his father could hold on until he returned.

When Jerry arrived, most of the Believers were together, but they felt weary and hopeless. Alina was nearly exhausted from using her powers to protect everyone from the fear and paralysis effects of the black smoke. Mega Fist and Johnny Bear suffered significant blood loss and possible infection from multiple zombie bites. Mr. Cream was still frozen in ice. Most importantly, Von was on the ground holding Blake, his lifeless best friend.

Jerry took a deep breath, realizing the situation was dire. In the best possible outcome, Jerry had enough energy to heal everyone and get rid of the black smoke, but he wouldn't have enough energy to fight Sanchez again. He was far too tired from his previous two battles with Sanchez, the U.S. military, and zombies. However, letting Sanchez escape and terrorize the rest of civilization was not an option. His father was also in danger, fighting against Sanchez as the last line of defense...what could Jerry do?

Von read Jerry's mind, stood up, and put his hand on Jerry's shoulder. Without saying a word, they both came to an agreement and began to take action. Von and Jerry took a few steps apart, but their backs were facing one another. Jerry now stood in front of his injured friends and Von stood alone, then they both began to summon their full power.

Their voices started as a low hum and continued to rise in unison. Von slowly pulled all the black smoke and negative energy into himself, transforming his body into pure darkness. Jerry gradually absorbed all the light and color in the area, soaking it inside his body to become the sun. Jerry and Von were feeding off each other and growing in power. When they both reached their limit, the entire battlefield turned gray, silent, and time stopped, as if they were in a void of nothingness. Then they both screamed and released their power.

Jerry unleashed a sphere of white light that engulfed the surrounding area, fully healing Blake and the Believers, along with most of the zombies. Soldiers who were thought to be lost forever miraculously came back to life as their rotting skin and bones reformed into their previously healthy selves.

Von charged in Sanchez' direction, using Jerry's energy burst as a boost to move faster than the speed of light. Mr. Miller had expended all his energy and Sanchez was about to deliver a killing blow, but Von instantly appeared in front of Sanchez and grabbed his skull and chest with both hands! Then he forced Sanchez away from Mr. Miller and opened a black hole! Sanchez immediately turned into dust and got sucked into the black hole, along with all the black smoke and negative energy Von had absorbed. The black hole closed, the white light dimmed, and both Von and Jerry fell unconscious.

Chapter 15:
DR. WANG

"IDIOTS! IDIOTS!"

Beep...beep...

"What were you thinking?"

Beep...beep...

"You two should have died! And don't get me started about Cynthia and the nukes!"

Beep...beep...

"Did you have to create a black hole, Von? It's a miracle you didn't die and kill everyone!"

Beep...beep...

"You Believers constantly defy everything we know about science and the universe...everything!"

Beep...beep...

Dr. Wang was complaining to herself while conducting tests and treating both Von and Jerry. They were unconscious and lying down in hospital beds at NASA headquarters in Florida. Agent X had brought all the Believers there, except Cynthia as she was still recovering at the Millers' house. Dr. Wang had treated astronauts before, so helping Von and Jerry was no different. However, both had expended far more energy than ever before and demonstrated abilities beyond anyone's expectations. Thankfully the other Believers were fully healed by Jerry's power, all of whom were waiting patiently with Agent X in another room. Since Leah was inside the NASA supercomputer, she was able to constantly monitor Von and Jerry's condition and relay information to his friends and family.

While treating the boys for 24 hours, Dr. Wang also reviewed video footage from their battle against Sanchez. Since the battle occurred at a presidential bunker, there were multiple videos to analyze, kindly provided by Agent X. Even when the black smoke was blocking the view of regular cameras, there were infrared cameras that revealed thermal images of everyone in battle. Leah excitedly worked with Dr. Wang to identify and discuss all the different powers as they were being used in the videos. Dr. Wang was both fascinated and annoyed by the Believers' powers and energy levels exhibited in the fight. The Believers' capabilities went against everything she learned as a doctor and scientist. The Believers were a phenomenon, and Dr. Wang could not accept it.

"Jerry, Von, and Cynthia transformed their own bodies into water, wind, shadow, light, and a dragon! That's whole-body metamorphosis! Cynthia manipulated the sky at a molecular level to stop nuclear bombs! Jerry instantly healed everyone and transformed REAL ZOMBIES back into functional people! Von traveled faster than the speed of light and killed Sanchez with a black hole! The Believers also have no real injuries or consequences; they're lying unconscious in beds but they're perfectly healthy! None of this makes any sense!"

Jerry finally woke up after hearing Dr. Wang's rant. She noticed and briefly explained where he was, then she was about to notify his friends and family to come in, but Jerry stopped her. He could feel her anxiety and wanted to help, so he engaged her in conversation.

"The others can wait; it'll give me a chance to gather my thoughts. In the meantime, tell me about you," Jerry requested.

"Me? What about me?"

"I know I aggravate you. I cost you time and money and challenge everything you know about our world."

"Yes, you do Jerry. Everything about you spits in the face of my entire life's work."

"But there's more to it than that...I can feel it," Jerry admitted.

"What could be more important than my life's work?" Dr. Wang sharply responded.

"I'm sorry, I know your work is important, but there's more to the story than you're telling me. Something deeper, from your past. We're all haunted by our past," Jerry admitted.

"Really? Your life seems amazing and perfect Jerry! You always win and you're happy and energetic all the time! What haunts you?"

"I killed Kevin and helped kill Sanchez. I failed to save 5,000 lives in the Indonesia earthquake. I couldn't save several people who were killed by Sanchez, Inferno, and Porter. Worst of all, every supervillain has done terrible things using powers that they gained from me...so I indirectly hurt everyone."

Dr. Wang was speechless, she could sense Jerry's sadness and feeling of guilt. She looked at Jerry for the first time with sincerity and trust. She always thought of him as a buffoon, stumbling his way through life with superpowers, but now she could see there was more to him than that. Since Jerry shared his past, she agreed to share hers.

"I wasn't like you Jerry...I wasn't special...just a regular girl born into a strict family that demanded far too much from me. They didn't see me as their daughter, they saw me as an asset to exploit."

"What do you mean?" Jerry asked.

"In my country, there are over a billion people all competing for the best schools, jobs, and money. Anyone who is less than top 10% is considered a failure. I barely made the cut, and yet I still disappointed my family."

"I'm sorry to hear that," Jerry said.

"Don't be, my family used me, they were jerks. They only saw me as money and a free ticket to America. At one point, they even wanted me to join the military! Me, a short and skinny girl with no muscle nor athletic background, that's ludicrous! And I actually considered it because I loved them! They never cared about my well-being, they only cared for themselves and what they could get out of me."

Jerry stayed quiet, not knowing how to respond, and waited for Dr. Wang to continue.

"When I first met you, I was so angry that you had superpowers and I didn't. I thought you were wasting your potential. I knew that if I had your powers, I could have easily been the top 1%, maybe even the best. I could have earned billions of dollars and made my family extremely happy!"

Jerry sighed with guilt, believing that Dr. Wang with her incredible intelligence probably could use his powers more effectively. Dr. Wang sensed Jerry's sympathy and cut him off before he could say something stupid to try and make her feel better.

"I know your powers are dangerous! I don't want them! I would probably use your powers to control everything and everyone around me, to make them perfect and conform to my view of the world. But I know I am wrong! You showed me how wrong I was about everything, and it made me mad! I hated my job and wanted to quit!"

Jerry desperately pleaded, "I'm sorry if I made you mad or hurt you."

"No, let me finish! It's more complicated than that! Your existence and everything you can do showed me that I have a lot more to learn. You pushed me to do more research and work harder to understand the ever-changing world of science and our universe. You opened my mind to new possibilities I had never even considered before. But most importantly, I am not alone! You have accidentally proven every scientist in history to be wrong! Now we all have a lot of learning and new work to do, and it's all thanks to you."

"Thank you for telling me that," Jerry smiled and expressed with gratitude.

"Of course. You also inspired me to cut off my negative family members for a while. I've given them plenty of money for years and they never thanked me nor respected me. Now I can work hard for myself instead of constantly trying to satisfy their greed."

Jerry sensed positive emotions coming from Dr. Wang; he felt happy and relieved that he was able to help her. Von woke up and abruptly announced, "Yep, I'm fine, thanks for asking. I love being woken up by a bunch of loudmouths. If you're both done talking, I'd like to get up and go home." Leah took that as her cue to alert everyone that the boys were awake, and they all rushed into the room. Dr. Wang promptly stepped aside as the Believers anxiously approached both Von and Jerry. They bombarded the boys with several questions, exclamations, hugs, and shared their experiences from the previous battle.

Dr. Wang watched with mostly happiness, but a tinge of jealousy and self-pity. The Believers acted as one big happy family, but Dr. Wang had never experienced anything like that before. Jerry was happy to be surrounded by his father, Agent X, and awesome Believers, but he felt Dr. Wang's confliction, so he stood up and called out to Dr. Wang who was hiding alone in the back of the room.

"Hey, Dr. Wang! Come over here!"

"Why? You are with family and friends. I'm only here monitoring you all because it's my job."

"You are part of this too! You're one of us!" Jerry declared.

"No, I am not. You are all heroes and I'm just..." Dr. Wang tried to finish her sentence, but her voice broke, and a tear came down her face.

"You've helped us several times! We couldn't have done any of this without you! You're family now!" Jerry proclaimed as he stood up from bed and walked towards Dr. Wang. He had his arms wide open and ready to hug her, but she brusquely replied, "Don't hug me."

"This is happening doc!"

"I don't need this."

"Yeah, you do!"

Dr. Wang looked around and realized her back was against the wall and she had nowhere to run. She saw Jerry closing in, so she stiffened up and closed her eyes. Jerry finally hugged her, and she felt surprisingly good! Jerry gave her a safe, warm hug and emitted tiny waves of positive energy to make her feel at ease. Then Jerry called out for everyone else to join and she was swiftly surrounded by lots of good people. Dr. Wang couldn't deny the wonderful feeling and accepted it...she was now part of the Believers family.

Chapter 16:
TIME FLIES

"IT'S BEEN A QUIET DAY!" JERRY EXCLAIMED.

"That's great to hear! I'm loving my new job at the hospital. It's a lot of work, but I'm learning and helping people every day," Cynthia acknowledged.

"Good to know. Can't wait to see you tonight and hear all about it. I gotta go, love you babe!"

"Love you too Jerry!"

The phone call ended, and they both continued with their day. Six months have passed since the death of Sanchez, and many things have changed. Jerry works for Agent X and the government as a national emergency specialist. When he's not handling such scenarios, he's training government personnel and Believers throughout the country. Any day without national emergencies is considered a "quiet day" for Jerry.

Cynthia continued improving her powers, trained a few times with Jerry, and found ways to read and learn faster, just like Jerry did to become a cop. She completed her nursing degree and now works full-time as a nurse in Miami while also studying to become a doctor. She even learned how to heal injuries with her powers and is studying how to heal diseases and other medical conditions.

Alina began working as a full-time therapist for emergency responders in Miami, using her mind powers to analyze and help them deal with mental trauma and other issues caused by their jobs. Von works as the top Police Lieutenant in Miami and responds to the most serious crimes such as shootings, homicides, robberies, and grand theft. Blake still plays for the NFL and continues breaking records for sacking quarterbacks. However, his fame as a superhero and NFL player have attracted companies to sponsor him and place him in TV and internet commercials.

Mr. Cream now travels around the world, making ice cream for adoring fans, but also using his ice powers to fight global warming and restore cold lands for polar bears, penguins, etc. Mega Fist and Johnny Bear joined the UFC global circuit, traveling together regularly to fight in high-stakes arena bouts against tough opponents. Mr. Miller continued his private business of selling boats in Miami. He enjoyed his short time as a superhero and hopes to never have to use his powers again.

Dr. Wang and NASA, along with Jackie the TV talk show hostess, are finishing the last touches on the humanoid robot body for Leah. They have performed numerous tests and feel she will be ready soon. Mrs. Miller and Cynthia's mother are working together to plan Jerry & Cynthia's wedding. They are doing daily research and getting together with their children once a week to make decisions. Jackie is also helping to fund and plan the wedding, thanks to Ryan arranging a deal for the wedding to be televised along with Leah's historic debut as the first humanoid robot.

As a pleasant surprise from the President of the United States, all the Believers received financial gifts for saving America and they used it in various ways. Von and Alina renovated Von's family home and they moved in together. Blake already had plenty of money from the NFL, so he donated his reward to charity. Mega Fist and Johnny Bear have their own families and kids, so they passed their rewards onto them. Mr. Cream invested his money into stocks of companies that fight against global warming. Cynthia donated her reward to her hard-working mother so she could live an easier life. Lastly, Jerry and Mr. Miller combined their rewards together to purchase a new home for Jerry, Cynthia, and Leah to live together.

***

Cynthia's mother, Pam Rodriguez, was very excited about her daughter's upcoming marriage to Jerry. To ensure a smooth family merger, she wanted to host a dinner at her home for the Millers. Keeping with Hispanic tradition, she decided to cook paella, a rice dish with a variety of meats, green beans, olive oil, rosemary, saffron, and artichoke. She also wanted to make a good first impression, so she wore light brown flats, white pants, and a gold short sleeve top. Cynthia and Jerry arrived early with all the ingredients to help Ms. Rodriguez cook, clean, and prepare her home for dinner.

Jerry wore black jeans, a gray dress shirt, and black boots. His outfit made him feel somewhat formal, but also comfortable and happy. Cynthia also wore dark pants and a gray long-sleeved top, but she did not feel happy, she felt nervous and worried. Jerry did not notice because they usually wear matching outfits when going out together. Cynthia had something important on her mind, something she never wanted to tell Jerry, but due to their upcoming marriage, it did not feel right to keep it a secret anymore. She hoped to tell him tonight but wasn't sure of the best time. Cynthia kept herself busy and thought all about it while helping her mother.

Mr. and Mrs. Miller finally showed up and Jerry opened the door for them. Mrs. Miller wore short beige heels, white pants, and a black top with short sleeves. Mr. Miller wore black dress shoes, khaki pants, and a white guayabera shirt. Jerry smiled and hugged his parents, then he led them to the living room where small appetizers and drinks were available. They all drank a glass of sangria (red wine with chopped fruits), along with croquetas, crackers, and guava jam.

Ms. Rodriguez was very gracious and thankful to the Millers for coming over. She felt indebted to them for helping Cynthia and embracing her as family, so now she wanted to do the same for Jerry and the Millers. She complimented each person, and they enjoyed pleasant small talk until they finished appetizers. Then they all sat down at the dining table for a traditional family dinner.

Before eating, Ms. Rodriguez offered a prayer. "Thank you, God, for granting us this opportunity to gather and enjoy food with our loved ones. Thank you for blessing our families and helping us through the good and bad times. Every time Jerry & Cynthia left to save the world, I prayed for their safe return, and you always brought them back. Now I hope they can be happily married and raise a family in a calm and peaceful world. Thank you for uniting our families and watching over us, amen."

Mr. Miller, who was very religious, smiled and appreciated her prayer. Everyone nodded their heads and then began to eat. After taking a few bites, various conversations ensued. They discussed weather, fishing, football, celebrities, movies, and TV shows. Once the main meal was finished, Mr. Miller brought up politics. Mr. Miller was mostly republican, but he became a little more liberal when his son gained superpowers, and he was curious about Cynthia and her mother's political views.

"Has anyone been following the news and politics lately?" Mr. Miller asked.

"I work a lot and usually don't pay much attention to the news," Ms. Rodriguez replied.

"Well, the president recently signed a new infrastructure bill into law," Mr. Miller said.

"That's a good thing, right?" Jerry chimed in.

"It depends on how you look at it. Republicans think the bill is too expensive, but democrats believe it's justified," Mr. Miller clarified.

"If the bill helps people, then we have to support it, right?" Jerry wondered.

"Life is not that simple, son. The bill is 2,701 pages long and costs $1.2 trillion, which means there's a lot of important details to consider. Plus, our country is already in serious debt that could take decades to pay off" Mr. Miller explained. Then he looked over to Cynthia and asked, "What do you think? Is the bill worth the price? Or should it have been revised and trimmed down before signing it into law?"

Cynthia was not paying attention and noticeably thinking about other concerns. Jerry squeezed her hand under the table to get her attention, then he quickly sent a telepathic message to her recapping what Mr. Miller was talking about and asking her. She gathered her thoughts, looked at Mr. Miller, and answered, "I think the bill was worth it because it'll help people and make our country better. America wastes money all the time. If the bill was rejected and sent back for revisions, the money would have been spent wastefully elsewhere."

"I understand your sentiment and I agree that certain elements of the bill are helpful. However, I read quite a bit of the bill and found lots of things that I don't believe are worth spending on. I think the bill could have easily been cut in half and still benefitted America." Mr. Miller argued.

"Sometimes you have to spend money, make sacrifices, and do things you're not proud of to help others!" Cynthia emotionally declared. Her response was personal, and everyone felt it. She immediately regretted her words and Mr. Miller didn't know how to react, feeling guilty that he accidentally triggered her. Mrs. Miller tried to change the topic, but Cynthia frantically apologized.

"I'm sorry, I didn't mean to yell at you Mr. Miller. You're a great dad and I value your opinions. I just...I just..." Cynthia's voice trailed off and she began crying. Everyone began asking if she was okay and she stuttered, "No...I'm not. I have something to tell you all. I couldn't go through with the wedding without my father, so I looked for him and..."

"You did what?! Why would you do that? He was a terrible father!" Ms. Rodriguez exclaimed.

"I know! You told me all the time, but you never explained why, and I didn't believe you! Leah felt bad and helped me find him. He just got out of jail, but the mafia was forcing him to work for them again, and I was desperate to have my father back in my life and at my wedding! So, I attacked the mafia and forced them to leave him alone, and I don't know if I did the right thing or not!" Cynthia announced with a high-pitched anxious voice.

Jerry was filled with both love and anger. He held her hand firmly, supporting her during such an emotional state, but also expecting a full explanation of everything she did with Leah, her father, and the mafia in the very near future. Mr. and Mrs. Miller felt sorry for Cynthia having to go through all of that. They liked her a lot and did not believe she deserved the stress and troubles of her father. Ms. Rodriguez, however, was shocked and furious!

"How could you do that without telling me?!"

"I don't know, it just happened! I didn't think Leah would find him so fast! I called him a few times in jail, and then he got out and said he needed my help! I'm sorry!" Cynthia pleaded.

"You had no right to go behind my back! Ugh...I knew this day would come! I tried everything to keep you away from him!"

"Why didn't you tell me more about him?"

"Because he's an idiot!" Ms. Rodriguez shouted, "I knew he would use you, especially with your superpowers!"

Knock, knock, knock. Everyone at dinner heard the door, then looked at Cynthia. Ms. Rodriguez put her palm to her forehead and proclaimed, "Ay, Dios mio! Did you tell him where we live?"

"Umm...maybe?"

"Ay! What am I going to do? I'm not ready for this!" Ms. Rodriguez panicked.

Knock, knock, knock...

While everyone else was caught up in the drama, Jerry decided to be a hero and teleport to the front door. He bravely opened it; he was fired up and ready for whoever was on the other side.

Chapter 17:
MR. RODRIGUEZ

"HELLO! IS THIS PAM AND CYNTHIA'S HOUSE?"

"Maybe, who are you?" Jerry replied.

"I'm Jack Rodriguez, Pam's husband and Cynthia's father! You're too young to be dating my wife though."

"Yep, you're right, I'm definitely not dating your wife."

"Haha! I was kidding! You must be Jerry, my future son-in-law!" Mr. Rodriguez proclaimed as he hugged Jerry with great enthusiasm and lifted him off the ground. Jerry felt like a toy being held by a giant. Mr. Rodriguez was large, hefty, and strong, wearing a black leather jacket with a white undershirt, blue jeans, and black boots. Cynthia smiled when she saw her father playing with Jerry, forgetting for a moment that her father was an ex-convict. After putting Jerry down, Mr. Rodriguez excitedly walked into his old home and announced himself to everyone in the dining room.

Pam was flustered, angry, embarrassed, and happy all at the same time. She was stunned that her husband was now back in her life after 15 years. She always assumed he would die or never return from his life of crime. Therefore, she never pursued a divorce. Now she had no clue what to say or do with her long-lost husband, so she followed her instincts and began screaming at him. The Millers were speechless and watched the scene unfold like audience members of a TV show.

"How could you use my daughter like that!?"

"Pam, my love, what do you mean? She called me! She wanted me back in her life!" Mr. Rodriguez defended himself.

"That's great! And the first thing you did was convince her to fight the mafia? What were you thinking!?"

"Baby, that's not how it happened! I would never put her in danger on purpose. I simply told her my situation, and she acted on her own."

"Jack! Don't act innocent! You knew exactly what she would do when you told her that! You almost got her killed!"

"Baby, come on, look at our daughter, she's all grown up! She's beautiful, strong, smart, and mature! She saved the world and she's getting married soon! She can make her own decisions now. You have to give her more credit."

"Oh no! Don't you dare do that Jack! Don't turn this on me! You don't get to flip the blame and charm your way out of this!"

"Pam, you know I love you. I am not blaming you nor Cynthia for anything. I am proud of you both and I'm sorry for being away so long."

"Ugh...I am not ready for this! You could've asked or warned me first!"

"I just got out of jail, and I couldn't stay away for another minute. 15 years was far too long, and we have so much to catch up on."

"It doesn't work that way, Jack! You can't just show up and expect everything to be back to normal! I don't even know if I want you back!"

"Pam, I know you better than anyone! Of course, you want me back! If you didn't, you would've grabbed your gun and shot me by now!"

"Mom! You have a gun?" Cynthia questioned her with disbelief.

"Yes! I bought it for her and taught her myself!" Jack proudly declared.

Pam began turning red, with both love and anger, and admitted, "Yes Cynthia, I have a gun, and maybe I do want you back Jack. But this was not the time for it! Do you know what I wanted tonight? A chance to show the Millers how much I appreciate them and prove that Jerry would be marrying into a normal, functional family. I just wanted a nice dinner, and maybe some karaoke later if people got bored. But you're a wild card that ruined everything!"

Pam was noticeably frustrated, and Jack surprisingly had nothing to say in return. Normally, Mrs. Miller would stay quiet and never interfere, but this moment of silence was the perfect opportunity to cheer Pam up, so she blurted out, "Nothing is ruined! We had an excellent dinner, and the night is young! I'm sure Mr. Rodriguez would like to sit down and get to know all of us, right? We can share stories and bond like family!"

Everyone stared at Mrs. Miller first, then back at Pam. Everyone wanted the same thing, a chance to relax and enjoy the rest of the night together. Everyone wanted a smooth wedding and having a successful family night was the first step towards that goal. Truthfully, Pam cared more for Cynthia than anyone else and when she looked into Cynthia's eyes, she knew exactly what Cynthia wanted. Pam took a deep breath and caved in, "Fine, take a seat Jack. I'll fix you a plate of food and a drink."

Jack happily sat down at the dinner table with everyone else waiting for him to speak. They all wanted to hear his story, and he was ready to reveal everything to prove his love to Pam and Cynthia. Jerry, however, was a bit skeptical. He hoped for Jack to be genuine and good, but he thought Jack was too cool and this was all too easy and convenient. Unfortunately, Jerry could not see into the future, so only time could tell if Jack was a good man or not. Hearing his story was the first step in the right direction, so Jerry reserved judgment and listened carefully.

"I never went to college. I was a blue-collar worker, doing manual labor jobs since I was 13 years old. I made enough money to take care of Pam and myself, but when Cynthia came along, things got tight."

"You turned to a life of crime because of me?" Cynthia asked with a tinge of guilt.

"No, it's not that simple," Jack reassured her, "I continued struggling, picking up more jobs, and working 16 hours a day, but it still wasn't enough. One day, I met a new client and did housework for him. He liked me a lot and paid well, then he introduced me to his friends and family, all of whom paid far more than my regular clients. They got me hooked and I became dependent on them for all my bills."

"I can understand," Mr. Miller chimed in, "In my business of selling boats, I've had questionable clients offer me unusually large amounts of money under the table. I had the luxury of saying *No*, but maybe you didn't."

Jack nodded and continued, "After running out of blue-collar work to do for them, they offered me criminal work that paid even more money. It wasn't the life I wanted, and Pam never approved, but supporting my family was my top priority, so I left after a heated argument to do what was best for them."

Cynthia teared up and burst out, "I remember that night! You left during dinner, and I was too young to understand why, so I cried for weeks!" Jerry held Cynthia and stared down her father with disapproval. *Even if Jack had to leave, he could've done it in a better way,* Jerry thought to himself. Jack knew what Jerry was thinking and avoided his eyes, trying to prevent conflict and finish his story.

"After a few years of work, the money was rolling in. I sent half of it to Pam and saved the rest for a better future. I wanted to leave the mafia and start my own business, but they didn't like that, so they set me up to get busted by the cops. It was an unspoken rule that any mafia members who became expendable would be framed and used as a scapegoat for serious crimes to save more important mafia members."

Jerry didn't believe his story and was about to speak up, but Mrs. Miller intervened, "I've watched documentaries like that on TV!" Then she looked at Pam and excitedly shouted, "That's why you never divorced him! You thought he was innocent! I knew it!"

Pam blushed, but Jerry was annoyed and interrogated his mother, "Wait, you knew about this?"

"Of course! You don't think I've talked with your future mother-in-law before? Don't forget that I also work as a magazine writer, so I research everything. Finding Jack's story was easy!" Mrs. Miller bragged. Jack nodded in appreciation and provided further details.

"My case was a done deal before I even got arrested. I was framed for murder and the cops knew I didn't do it; my personality and background didn't match the gruesomeness of the crime.

When I saw the pictures, I almost puked! But the evidence was perfect and all pointing to me, so I pleaded guilty for a reduced sentence and worked hard to get out early."

Jerry still wasn't completely convinced of the story and Jack sensed it, so he added, "Look, I get that I'm not innocent. I didn't kill anyone, but I did commit other crimes and felt like I deserved the punishment, so I stuck it out without question. I volunteered for every clean job in prison and did everything to impress the jailers. Before getting out, the mafia began threatening me to work for them again. Luckily, Cynthia found me and saved my life! I wouldn't be here without her, and I'll spend the rest of my life making it up to her and everyone she loves."

While Jerry remained skeptical, he read the room and realized everyone else believed in Jack. Pam was love-stricken and viewed her husband as a whole new man. Cynthia wanted a father so badly that she was willing to overlook his past and begin building a new father-daughter relationship with him. Mrs. Miller loved soap operas, so she viewed Jack as a former villain transforming into a hero to support his family. Mr. Miller, usually the most conservative and strict person in the room, forgave Jack's previous mistakes since he had already served time in prison. Therefore, Jerry concluded that he should give Jack a chance to redeem himself as a civilian and family man.

The rest of the night went well. Everyone shared fun stories and laughed together. They ate dessert and exchanged small gifts to commemorate the upcoming wedding. Then they played party games involving cards, questions, and dice. Everyone had a great time and the night ended with everyone hugging and saying their goodbyes. Jack spent his first night back home with Pam, reminiscing about the past and planning for the future. The Millers went home to sleep. Jerry and Cynthia, however, had a lot to talk about at their new home.

When they arrived back home, they changed into sleeping clothes and jumped into bed. Jerry contacted Leah through his phone and put her on loud speaker. Now that everyone was connected and comfortable, Jerry was ready to hear the full story of how Cynthia helped her father with the mafia. Cynthia and Leah had worked together during the event, so they both agreed to tell Jerry all the details.

Chapter 18:
CYNTHIA & LEAH VS. THE MAFIA

"YOU FOUND HIM?" CYNTHIA GASPED.

"Yeah, it was easy!" Leah confirmed.

"I wasn't expecting this, I thought it would take months!"

"Did you forget that I live inside a NASA supercomputer? He was easy for me to find, especially since he's in prison."

"What!? Are you serious Leah?"

"Yep, here's the phone number."

"I'm not ready for this, it's happening so fast! And why prison? What kind of father is he?" Cynthia continued muttering questions uncontrollably.

Leah soon cut her off, "Mom! Relax, you've got this. Call him up and I'll be listening; I'll research anything important or fishy."

Cynthia smiled and replied, "I'm still not used to being called *Mom*, but you're an amazing daughter, Leah. I'll toughen up and call my dad now."

Cynthia took a deep breath, gathered her thoughts, and called the phone number. When the operator first answered, he explained that normally people cannot call prisoners directly and must wait for prisoners to call them. However, Cynthia revealed herself to be a superhero and explained her desire to find her long lost father, then the operator placed her on hold for a few minutes. When the operator returned, he forwarded her call to the warden, the head

116

supervisor of the prison. It turned out that the warden was a fan of superheroes and loved Cynthia's story, so the warden found her father in prison and arranged a private phone call.

When Cynthia's father, Mr. Rodriguez, answered the phone, she was filled with joy. He sounded like a kind and fun person, definitely worth reconnecting with. He apologized for being absent and promised he would be home soon. All was well until he mentioned the mafia threatening him to work for them upon his release from prison. Wanting to be a hero and desperate to help her father return home, Cynthia begged him to give her information about the mafia member who was threatening him. Leah, who was listening to the phone call, began researching and quickly found the mafia member's home. His name was Cesar Cuzinsky, and Cynthia was ready to pay him a visit.

***

"Wait a second!" Jerry interrupted the girls' story, "Why didn't you all ask me for help with Cesar Cuzinsky and the mafia?"

"Are you crazy Dad?" Leah blurted out of the cellphone.

"What do you mean? I could've totally helped!"

"No way! You're a cop and a federal agent!"

"So what?"

"Attacking the mafia would get you in big trouble!"

Jerry wanted to argue back, but he paused to think. Cynthia took the opportunity to explain a few things.

"Jerry, you took an oath and signed contracts to become an official cop and federal agent. The mafia would've ruined your career if you got involved. I, on the other hand, did not sign anything. I unofficially work as a superhero during emergencies, but it's not my main career."

"So, what are you trying to say?" Jerry asked with a confused tone.

"Mom's a vigilante!" Leah shouted.

"Technically, most of the Believers are, except you and Von," Cynthia clarified.

Jerry was caught by surprise; he never considered how different he was compared to most of the Believers, including his future wife.

Jerry always knew he wanted to be a hero and did everything to achieve that goal. Meanwhile, Von only became a cop because of Jerry and his father, everyone else had their own jobs and dreams outside of being heroes.

While Jerry pondered all of this, Cynthia smiled and declared, "I like being a vigilante, has a nice ring to it."

"And I'm your sidekick!" Leah exclaimed.

Jerry laughed, "Okay vigilantes, finish telling me your story."

✳✳✳

When Cynthia arrived at the front gate of the mafia mansion, she stared with disbelief at the luxurious home. There were two large, statuesque fountains with crystal blue water shooting out. Beautiful flowers, tall palm trees, and small greenery encompassed the front yard, including wide tile pathways for people and cars to travel up to and around the home. The home itself was two stories with white walls, a gray roof, extravagant windows, and about fifteen rooms. Even though there was a solid black front gate, the rest of the house was surrounded by a vast forest.

There was a keypad and speaker, but before calling the homeowner, Cynthia took a moment to concentrate and scan the area with her powers. She quickly discovered multiple guards with guns hiding in the forest trees. Keeping that information in mind, she finally called Cesar Cuzinsky.

"Hi, is Mr. Cuzinsky home?"

"Who's asking?" Cesar questioned with a grumpy voice.

"I'm the daughter of Jack Rodriguez and I've come here to make a request."

"Jackie boy? Haven't seen him in years, sorry toots."

"He called me from prison and told me you were after him, so I came here to make a deal with you."

"No deal. He either comes to work for me or he dies," Cesar concluded.

"What? Hell no!" Cynthia exclaimed.

Cesar ended the call and the gate remained closed, so Cynthia decided to open it herself. She charged up her hands with electrical energy and grabbed the gate, then she ripped it apart at the

118

molecular level! She repeatedly pulled pieces of metal off the gate, enough to create an open space and walk through.

Upon entry, gunshots broke the sound barrier as bullets bombarded her. However, none of them touched her. She had molecular webs around her body that stopped the bullets inches away from her. Dozens of bullets quickly stacked up, almost making it difficult to see through. She exploded with anger, releasing a surge of energy that bounced all the bullets back at their attackers! Her bullets, however, were purposely slower with the intention of causing harm, but not killing the guards.

Once the guards were disabled, Cynthia walked forward without interruption. She passed the serene water fountain, walked through breezy pathways, and reached the front door. Taking a moment to breathe, she decided to politely knock. Surprisingly, a timid young man answered.

"Hello ma'am, can you please leave?"

"Are you kidding me? No!" Cynthia reacted sharply.

"It's my first day on the job and I don't want any trouble."

"Then tell your boss I need to talk with him!"

"He already said *No* and there are lots of angry men behind me that are ready to kill you."

"I don't care! I'm gonna blast the door soon if you don't open up!" Cynthia shouted impatiently.

The young man turned around to his friends and pleaded, "Guys, can we let her inside? She's gonna blow the door open anyway and that'll just make the boss angrier."

Cynthia heard a gunshot on the other side of the door and the young man scurried away whining, "I'm sorry!"

Cynthia sighed, feeling pretty sure what was coming next. She took a deep breath, braced herself, and the villains predictably fired everything they had at the door. Bullets and missiles destroyed the entire front entrance and bombarded Cynthia. Smoke and debris shot out everywhere and loud *BOOM* sounds echoed throughout the mansion.

Cesar Cuzinsky was surely proud of his men, thinking they had eliminated the threat, but he was sorely mistaken. Cynthia surprisingly appeared right in front of him! Cesar thought he was safe inside his secret panic room, a heavily reinforced location hidden beneath the mansion. This room was built to be indestructible and can only be opened from the inside once it's locked. Now Cesar was alone with Cynthia, and he had no guards or anything to protect himself from her. Cynthia grinned, "Now can we talk?"

Cesar nervously backed up and inquired, "How did you find me?"

"My daughter is really good with computers, and I purposely scared you into your panic room."

"How did you get inside here?"

"I sensed your energy and teleported right to you; superpowers are really helpful."

Cesar grunted with frustration and yelled, "This changes nothing! I won't help you with your father!"

"Why not?" Cynthia demanded.

"If anyone finds out that I gave into you, then everyone will think I'm soft and want the same treatment."

"And what if I kill you?" Cynthia added.

"You won't, you're a superhero! People like you never kill."

Cynthia suddenly erupted with rage, "If you won't leave my father alone, then I'll take everything away from you!"

Cynthia's whole body began vibrating and surging with energy, then the room began to shake, and Cesar fell onto the ground. Frightened for his life, he begged for mercy, "Please stop whatever you are doing!"

"No! You asked for this, and you'll pay for it! Raaaaaaaahh!!!" Cynthia screamed and released massive shockwaves that caused an earthquake! The entire mansion rumbled and began falling apart! Cesar found an automatic rifle and desperately held the trigger, firing all his bullets at Cynthia in the hopes of stopping her madness. Unfortunately, the bullets stopped short, suspended in mid-air due to her molecular webbing. Feeling helpless, Cesar covered his head, closed his eyes, and cowered in the fetal position.

After a minute or two, Cesar felt warm and opened his eyes to an unbelievable sight. His entire mansion was destroyed, and he was standing inside an open crater! He saw rays of sunlight and felt wind blowing past him through his crumbled home. This event seemed like an act of God, the wrath of nature and the universe, but it was merely the will of a young woman doing everything to save her father's life. After witnessing the devastation, Cesar accepted that he was wrong.

"I give up! I'll erase your father from my list...he's a free man."

Cynthia beamed with joy while all the injured guards and maids began arguing and asking what happened to the mansion. Many earthquakes last only a few seconds, but Cynthia purposely controlled her power and created a slow-acting earthquake, allowing everyone time to escape. As a result, nobody died, and Cynthia got what she wanted...her father's freedom.

***

"Wow, that's one heck of a story! I can't believe you did it all alone!" Jerry expressed disbelief and admiration.

"Hey! I was there too...kind of." Leah chirped as if she felt left out.

"I know Leah. I'm grateful that you helped me as much as you did. You're the best daughter ever," Cynthia admitted.

"Thank you! At least someone gets me!" Leah shouted with an annoyed tone.

"Hey, I know how awesome you are," Jerry acknowledged, "that's why I'm working extra hours with NASA and Jackie to make sure your robot body is ready soon. Then I can kick your butt in bowling, soccer, and video games!"

"No way! I'm taking you down, Dad! And if I lose, I'll team up with Mom and we'll both beat you!" Leah retorted.

"That's right! Mother and daughter power!" Cynthia cheered.

Jerry laughed and looked forward to being a real family with Cynthia as his wife and Leah as his robot daughter. However, he had one last question for Cynthia.

"I just thought about your mafia story, and something is bothering me. How do you know that Cesar won't come after you, your family, or us in the future? What if he wants revenge?"

"Oh yeah, I forgot the best part! I used my powers to put his mansion back together!"

"What? How?"

"We've been together a long time, Jerry. I've learned a lot from you and trained myself as well. I've nearly mastered my molecular powers, so it's easy for me to put molecules back in their original position."

"Can you put anything back together, even a person?" Leah questioned.

"I think so, but I'd have to know the person really well and it would take a lot of energy to do it." Cynthia answered.

Leah went dead silent,

...

as if the phone died.

...

After a few more seconds,

...

Leah finally spoke.

"Mom...you know me really well...how come you never tried...putting me back together?"

Leah's sadness and disappointment penetrated Cynthia's soul. Her confidence and happiness shattered into pieces on the ground. Her heart broke and she temporarily stopped breathing. She cringed in pain, suddenly remembering the moment on the boat when Leah was killed by a laser through her back. She remembered watching her limp and lifeless body, feeling powerless and unable to help.

Jerry could feel Cynthia's pain and knew exactly what she was going through. He experienced the same trauma many days and nights after Leah died in his arms. Jerry held Cynthia close for support, but he chose to stay quiet, knowing that she had to work through the pain alone in order to accept and overcome it.

Soon she gasped for air, looked worriedly at Jerry's phone, and then explained everything to Leah.

"When your accident happened, I wasn't ready yet, I hadn't completed my training. Even now, it's still very risky because I've never built a person before, and I don't have your old body to work with. What if I make a mistake and you get hurt or die? Your father and I would never forgive ourselves. Your cancer also complicates things because I only knew you with cancer, so I don't know if I can remake you without cancer. I'm sorry Leah..."

Both girls were quiet and somber for a bit, absorbing everything they'd just discussed. Eventually, Jerry chimed in, "Leah, remember that your mother and I love you very much. We want you to be safe, so we'll never risk your life on experimental treatment. We're also doing everything we can to make sure your future robot body is even better than your old body. That way you'll at least have a chance of beating me at all my favorite games."

"Hey, I don't need to cheat to win! But I'll take the robot body if it has cool features, and it better come with weapons! I'm going with you guys on all your superhero adventures!" Leah exclaimed.

Jerry and Cynthia smiled, feeling more confident after the conversation. They believed their love for each other, and Leah, could get them through any future challenges. They were finally ready to be married and live happily ever after, as a family.

Chapter 19:
WEDDING OF THE CENTURY

"IT'S BEEN MONTHS SINCE WE'VE HAD ANY superhero incidents." Cynthia said.

"Isn't that a good thing?" Alina asked.

"Of course! But I hope nothing bad happens today. I don't want anyone to get hurt."

"Don't worry about that Cynthia! Today is your wedding day! The rest of the Believers can handle anything that comes up."

"And what about Leah? I hope she's ready for today. I haven't heard from her in weeks."

"Dr. Wang told you that NASA needed her to run final tests for her new robot body. I'm sure she'll be ready on time, or else Jackie will have a fit!" Alina exclaimed.

"Speaking of Jackie, I can't believe she organized such a crazy event! 4,000 people attending our wedding is WAY too much, and it's being televised!"

"What did you expect? Jackie is a TV show host, and you all are global superheroes! You saved the entire world from a nuclear war! Important people, governments, and organizations are supporting this event. This will be the wedding of the century!" Alina proclaimed.

"You're right, but I feel bad for my father. He wants to keep a low profile and doesn't want everyone to know about his criminal past."

"Your dad will be fine! Stop worrying about everyone else! This is YOUR wedding day! Be selfish for once!"

"You're right," Cynthia admitted, "I should be enjoying myself instead of worrying about everyone else. I'm sorry if I'm being annoying. I know you'd love a crazy wedding like this."

"Probably! But Von wouldn't, he'd be working as head of security and using his mind powers to scan every person for possible threats. He takes his police job WAY too seriously."

"I can't blame him! Someone has to protect my best friend. I love you, Alina. Thanks for being here for me."

"No problem, what are best friends for? Anyway, no more mushy stuff. Time to walk down the aisle! You got this girl!"

Cynthia stood up from her make-up chair, took a deep breath, and walked out of the room. She was standing in a candle-lit hallway with religious portraits decorating the walls. The wedding was being held in one of the largest temples in the world, able to accommodate all 4,000 attendees. Most people had to catch planes to reach the temple. However, a few high-profile guests, including some of the world's most popular celebrities and world leaders, had to be teleported into the event by Jerry due to time restraints and safety reasons.

There were endless rows of benches inside the temple, where everyone was seated and waiting for the wedding to begin. Everyone wore wedding-appropriate clothing, but there was a woman outside the temple who sold inexpensive shawls to people in case they needed to cover up more. The temple had a very high ceiling with stone columns for support and statues of angels and other religious figures.

Jerry was standing at the altar with the priest. Jerry wore a standard black tuxedo, but he also added a white gold insignia letter *B* on the left side of his chest to represent the Believers. Alina texted Jerry that Cynthia was ready. He happily gave everyone a thumbs-up, signaling that the wedding would begin shortly.

Soon wedding music filled the temple, with a full chorus and a mixture of bells, an organ, and a piano. The bride & groom parties were ready to play their part. Alina, wearing a yellow dress with curly red hair, walked down the aisle with Von, who wore a dark blue jacket and pants with a white dress shirt and black tie.

Next was Blake, who wore a similar outfit to Von, but he was not alone. Next to him was a fiery hot young woman with dirty blonde hair wearing a long dark red dress. Since Blake was a famous NFL football star, a few people cheered in the crowd, and others could be heard whispering about the woman being a cheerleader from his team.

Second to last, but arguably one of the most important, Leah walked down the aisle alone featuring her brand-new robot body. It looked so real that people could barely tell the difference. Her robot body had the appearance of a 15-year-old girl with shoulder-length brunette hair and a subtle long beige dress. All video cameras were focused on her, and photographers snapped several pictures from all angles. When Leah reached the altar, she stopped and turned around to look at all 4,000 guests. The wedding music ended, and she gave a short speech.

"I know many of you are here to see me, the first ever humanoid robot, and I know you have plenty of questions. But today is all about Jerry & Cynthia, my loving parents and saviors of the world. All of us would not be here today without their help, so please honor them on their wedding day, the most important day of their lives. Thank you."

Leah walked to her seat, and everyone tried asking questions, but Jackie's team of helpers calmed everyone down and reminded everyone that the bride was waiting. The temple was now silent and still in honor of the bride. When Cynthia finally appeared, she bedazzled everyone with her lavender wedding dress, silver slippers, long brunette hair, a tiara & necklace made of diamonds, and perfectly tanned skin.

Jerry smiled widely when he saw his future wife. Cynthia smiled back and extended her arm for her father. Her father wore a traditional white dress shirt with a black tie, jacket, and pants. Cynthia's mother was proud of them both and shed a tear as they walked down the aisle together. Jerry's parents were speechless and in awe, never thinking this day would come. They always wanted Jerry and Cynthia to get married, but feared their superhero lives would never allow it to happen. Mrs. Miller whispered, "Beautiful," as Cynthia walked by. Many people expressed similar emotions and sentiments, for which Cynthia smiled and nodded at individuals to assure them that she saw and understood them on a personal level.

When Cynthia reached the altar, her father handed her to Jerry and sat down while the soon-to-be married couple stood in front of the priest. The priest performed a traditional religious ceremony that took 30 minutes, filled with scripture reading and blessings from the bible. Unlike many young couples today, Jerry and Cynthia enjoyed the ceremony. It made them feel the gravity and significance of their pairing, similar to the responsibility of using their superpowers to help the world. They genuinely wanted the support of God in their future journey together.

At the end of the ceremony, Jerry & Cynthia shared their heartfelt vows and promised to love and honor each other, then they sealed it with a kiss. Family and friends were overjoyed, and tons of confetti rained down from above as the newlywed couple made their way back down the aisle together.

Everyone moved to the reception, which was being held outside in a vast field with grass, trees, tables & chairs, tents, buffet style dining, a performance stage, and a cool breeze under sunny skies. Jerry, Cynthia, Leah, Von, Alina, Blake, and his cheerleader friend spent the first hour taking numerous pictures with thousands of people. They traveled around the reception having quick snacks and drinks from the buffet throughout their photography expo. They even conducted their first dances together with family on stage, leading to more pictures, tears, and fun.

Afterward, they sat down and relaxed while watching multiple events on stage. Jackie's team had musical bands, professional dancers, and even danger acts with fire and knife-throwing. Everyone enjoyed the festivities and during breaks, Jerry had a chance to interact with a few memorable people from his past.

First, he found his favorite high school teacher, Mrs. Perse. She congratulated him for marrying Cynthia, who was also her student. Jerry appreciated her words, but he also apologized to her and explained how he felt guilty about scaring and annoying her in the classroom. She kindly shrugged off his words, acknowledging that Jerry's time in high school was more confusing than most teenagers, especially when still learning about his new powers and how to live a balanced life. Jerry gave her a hug and thanked her for being the best teacher he ever had.

Next up was Ryan, his long-time best friend. They gave each other a bro hug, including a loud high-five, and talked about the good ole days. Ryan told Jerry that he helped Jackie select some of the songs and performances.

Jerry excitedly affirmed, "I knew that was you! Half of those would never be in a normal wedding!"

Ryan laughed and replied, "Yep, I told Jackie that we couldn't accept a boring wedding, especially with the President of the United States and other important guests here. We had to give them a surprise, something worth talking about."

"That's awesome, thanks a lot Ryan. We really gotta go surfing sometime, it's been way too long."

"Agreed! You should bring Cynthia and Leah too. By the way, Leah's new robot body won't rust or short-circuit in the water, will it? Can she even swim?"

"Bro! Way too soon! You can't be cracking those jokes yet, at least until we know the answers."

"I'm kidding Jerry. I'm sure Leah will be able to live a completely normal life and do all the same activities as everyone else. Anyway, you gotta meet my new girl. We just started dating recently and she does everything for me, she's the best! I think she might be the one."

"That's great to hear Ryan, we'll definitely hit the beach together soon. I gotta go talk to some other guests, I'll see you around."

"Later bro."

Lastly, Jerry & Cynthia met up together and mingled with their family, friends, and fellow Believers. The Millers and Rodriguez families were all together, drinking and laughing as if they'd known each other for years. When the newlyweds arrived, they started making jokes about wanting grandkids. Jerry & Cynthia gave them all hugs and nodded their heads, but they weren't planning on having kids anytime soon since they just got Leah physically back in their lives.

Nurse Anne and Mr. Hamel found the couple and wished them a happy marriage while offering them plenty of advice. Mega Fist introduced his American wife and two infant daughters to Jerry & Cynthia. Johnny Bear introduced his Korean wife and 4-year-old son as well. Feeling happy and energetic, Jerry played with all the kids for a bit, using his powers to impress and entertain them. Cynthia smiled at the sight, knowing that Jerry would be a great father for Leah and any future children they have together.

Mr. Cream conducted his dance performance with wildly colorful ice cream flying into bowls. Thousands of guests lined up to grab their bowls and enjoy the various flavors, all of which were rich and delicious. Alina approached Cynthia and joked that she needed all the hookups and contacts for her future wedding with Von. Von put his arm around Jerry and boisterously announced, "We're not here to talk about us and a future wedding, we're here to talk about Jerry! Time to make a toast!"

"Nope! This is my time baby! I got the best story to share with everyone, and it involves both Jerry and Von!" Blake shouted and stood up, cutting off Von and stealing the spotlight. Everyone got quiet and paid close attention. Both Jerry and Von were anxious, wondering what story Blake would tell and listened closely.

"In Jerry's early years as a hero in training, he was very eager to learn everything and improve himself. Luckily, Von loved that about Jerry and tried to coach him on everything related to fighting and survival. It's probably why they're best friends today. HOWEVER, Von was also very competitive and didn't like losing!"

The crowd chuckled, many feeling they could easily relate to that.

"One day, Von thought it was a great idea to teach Jerry how to swordfight! Now I know some of you are scared that someone will get stabbed in this story, but I promise you that swords were the least of Jerry's worries. In fact, he may have been better off with a sword cut!"

Cynthia opened her mouth with surprise, not knowing anything about this story and wanting to hear more.

"So, Jerry and Von grab their swords and start going at it. Von chose a massive two-handed sword, wanting to prove how big and bad he was, swinging a huge weapon that could slay a dragon! But

Jerry chose a short sword and was fast as lightning! He got numerous small hits on Von and made him look like a fool!"

Mega Fist and Johnny Bear were giggling loudly at the idea of Von, the super cop, losing to Jerry's tiny sword.

"If you all know Jerry well, he's the nicest guy around and would never hurt his friends. So Jerry used the flat side of his sword when hitting Von, never drawing blood and only hurting his pride. Eventually, Von lost his cool, charged forward, and football-tackled Jerry to the ground!"

The crowd gasped in shock, sitting on the edge of their seats, and waiting for the ending.

"The good news was nobody got stabbed. The bad news was when Von tried pulling Jerry up onto his feet, they realized Jerry's wrist was broken! It was black & blue and swelling up fast! Thankfully, Jerry had superpowers and healed himself quickly, but Von felt bad and apologized. Jerry played it cool though; he never complained and told Von not to worry about it. The best part about the whole thing was that I had front row seats and watched it all go down! I tried telling them not to do it, but they didn't listen, and I got a great story out of it! Thanks Jerry and Von, you guys are the best friends ever!"

Everyone stood up to applaud and cheer as Blake walked over and gave a wide hug to his best friends. Everyone enjoyed the story, and moments later, Alina began tapping her glass with a fork to get everyone's attention. She too wanted to share a tale about her newlywed best friend.

"Hello everyone, my story is about a younger Cynthia who had friends over for her birthday. Do you think her parents were home? Nope! You all know what that means! Cynthia threw a wild party!"

"Woot woot!" Audience members hollered in appreciation. Alina waited for everyone to calm down, then she continued.

"You all know I'm kidding right? Cynthia was always very innocent, even on her birthday. However, she wanted to make new friends during her first year of high school, so she invited a variety of people, including a few shady ones. I watched everyone and tried my best to keep Cynthia out of trouble, but she made it difficult! Can you believe what she did that night?"

Alina paused for dramatic effect, then she revealed, "Cynthia ate special brownies!"

The audience lost it and began cackling like hyenas. They never expected Cynthia to do anything like that. After the audience's uproar finished, Alina unveiled the next part.

"In Cynthia's defense, she had no idea what special brownies were, but she definitely regretted it. After eating only one, she was physically and mentally gone! She couldn't walk or talk! We were all playing card games and she struggled for five minutes just to put down a single card! Eventually she quit the game and passed out on the couch!"

The audience started laughing again and Cynthia turned bright red with embarrassment. Alina saw her best friend's face, but she loved the attention from the crowd and had to finish the story.

"That's not even the best part! She woke up later and everyone wanted to play *Spin the Bottle*. So we started playing and whenever the bottle landed on someone, you had to kiss them. However, Cynthia was way too shy to kiss a random guy. So, when it was her turn to kiss someone, she surprised everyone and kissed me on the lips!"

The audience died laughing and both Jerry and Von's mouths were gaping open, completely shocked by everything they heard. Alina knew Cynthia wanted to kill her for sharing all that, so Alina provided positive closure.

"I want you all to remember that Cynthia is the most loving and caring girl I know. She may have been wild that one night, but she's been reliable and responsible her entire life. When she gained superpowers, she literally saved the world! She's never done anything selfish or harmful to anyone. She treats everyone with respect. I cherish her dearly and feel lucky to be her best friend. Everyone please give her a round of applause! This is her wedding night, and she deserves all our love!"

All 4,000 guests gave her a standing ovation. They celebrated and cheered for her as if she were a queen. Cynthia looked around and cried tears of joy; she now felt like a true hero. Alina walked up to her and hugged her tightly. All TV cameras were focused on that scene, and billions of people around the world were touched by what they saw.

Jackie's TV show ratings were shooting through the roof! This wedding achieved results beyond her expectations. However, Jackie was now ready for the finale. She announced that they would go to a commercial break and return shortly for Leah's first interview as a humanoid robot.

Chapter 20:
THE WORLD MEETS LEAH, THE ROBOT

"LADIES AND GENTLEMEN, THE MOMENT you've all been waiting for has arrived! Welcome to the first ever interview with a real humanoid robot!"

4,000 wedding guests cheered as Leah walked up onto the stage of the reception area. Her brunette hair and long beige dress flowed so naturally that people had trouble believing she was a robot. With everyone staring at her, she felt the weight of the world upon her shoulders, as if she needed to prove that she was a real person and more than a robot. She smiled and spontaneously performed a short dance. She put her hands together and did circular motions while swaying her body left-to-right, then she hopped up and down a few times and ended with a thumbs up to the audience.

Everyone lost their minds, clapping endlessly at the surprise dance and a break from the formal wedding event. Leah waved and thanked everyone, then she sat down in a comfortable chair next to Jackie, the TV show hostess. Jackie was wearing a bright sky-blue dress that matched her delightful persona. She was ecstatic, knowing that this interview would certainly put her in the history books. After everyone finished applauding, she began the interview.

"Leah! Thank you for joining us today! Tell us how you feel."

"I feel like a million bucks! I'm living in the real world and being watched on live TV!"

"Yes! Leah, you're here with us now and we are forever grateful. I know your struggles and what you've been through, but many people have no clue. Please explain your journey and how you got here."

Leah looked at everyone, gathered her thoughts, and explained. "I was born as a regular girl, but I lived as an orphan without family, surrounded by strangers and struggling to survive with cancer. I didn't want to live, I felt like I had no purpose and was waiting to die."

"Whoa, that's heavy! But you weren't like that when I first met you," Jackie pointed out, "You were playful and happy."

"That's because of Jerry & Cynthia; they found me at age 12 and completely changed my life. I learned a lot from them, and they made me feel like family, filling a hole in my heart and giving me a reason to live."

"That's beautiful! Everyone give a round of applause for Jerry & Cynthia!" Jackie requested and the audience responded with celebratory handclapping. Jerry & Cynthia stood up and waved at everyone, thanking them for their kindness. Leah smiled happily at Jerry & Cynthia and Jackie noticed their strong connection; she wanted the audience to see it too.

"Leah, are Jerry and Cynthia special to you?" Jackie asked.

"Yes," Leah answered softly, "I consider them my parents."

"Do you want them up here with you?"

"Yes!"

"All right! Jerry and Cynthia, come on up!"

The audience hailed Jerry and Cynthia as they gracefully approached the stage. Leah hugged them both with relief, not wanting to do the interview alone. Cynthia caringly placed her hand upon Leah's face; she was proud of her daughter for everything she endured. Jerry spread his arms and held both Cynthia & Leah close to his chest, demonstrating strength and love for his family. Numerous flashing lights and camera shudders captured the emotional moment. Everyone soon sat down again, and Jackie continued the interview.

"So you were a 12-year-old girl, born and raised in America, and now you're a humanoid robot. How did that happen?"

"I was lucky enough to gain a superpower, the ability to move through objects. At first, it was silly and fun, great for pulling pranks on other orphan kids. I would walk through walls, into other kids' bedrooms, and make ghost noises or knock things on the ground, then hurry back to my room before getting into trouble. After meeting Jerry & Cynthia, however, I learned more about my powers and realized I could leave my own body."

"Wow, that's wild Leah! So, I assume you left your original body because you were dying of cancer, right? Or is there more to the story?"

"It wasn't that simple," Leah replied, "I loved my body and didn't want to leave. Jerry gave me hope when he found a way to stop my cancer from killing me. He couldn't cure me though, so I still felt pain and side-effects of cancer. I was always tired and endured repeated diarrhea and vomiting, but at least I was alive! I wanted to fight it and find a cure eventually, but fate had a different plan."

"What do you mean?" Jackie questioned.

"Well, there was an evil man mind-controlling people to do terrible things. He mind-controlled our friend, Laserpoint, and shot me in the back with a laser on my 13th birthday. I was dying and my body instinctively activated my power and moved my mind into Jerry's cellphone. It was a freak accident, and it took me months to figure out where I was and how to communicate with my friends."

Everyone was speechless and listening closely to Leah's unbelievable tale, so she continued.

"Eventually Jerry and Cynthia introduced me to Dr. Wang, the best scientist at NASA. She worked tirelessly to build my robot body; I owe everything to her. Thank you, Dr. Wang!" Leah happily shouted and waved at Dr. Wang, who was sitting in the audience. Cynthia nodded in approval and Jerry gave Dr. Wang a big thumbs-up.

Everyone immediately gave a standing ovation to Dr. Wang, who remained seated as expected of her guarded nature. But she did smile and shed a tear; she never dreamed of receiving such appreciation for her work. After the audience sat down, Jackie chimed in.

"So now that we know how you got here, tell us more about your robot body."

"It's amazing! I can walk, run, and do everything like a normal girl. I can feel the wind blowing, the warmth of the sun, and the cool touch of night. When I splash my face with water, it feels refreshing and softens my skin. When I lay down in a bed of flowers and stare at the sky, it gives me a sense of freedom and comfort."

"Wow Leah, you're the real deal! I'm so happy for you. But tell me what happens if you get injured."

"My body has tiny nanites that repair any injuries."

"Can you show us an example?" A random man shouted from the audience.

"How?" Leah asked with an annoyed tone as she looked toward the man.

"Administer a cut to show the healing process," the man answered coldly.

Leah became furious; this man commanded her as if she was a toy or machine to be tested. She lost her temper, leapt out of her chair, and yelled, "No! I won't hurt myself for your amusement! I'm a real person and I feel pain like anyone else!"

Jerry stood up to support his daughter, and Cynthia angrily stared at Jackie. In response, Jackie stood up, sneered at the man, and announced, "We will not tolerate any interruptions from the crowd. You are lucky to attend this historic event. Do not forget that Jerry's family and the Believers saved all of Earth from a nuclear war, as well as other previous global threats. This interview will continue with integrity and respect. Any further outbursts will result in immediate dismissal."

That man stayed silent for the rest of the evening. Jerry and Leah both sat down and awaited Jackie's next question.

"I wanted to dive into your emotions and heart, but we all clearly just witnessed that you are as human as everyone else! Kudos to you girl!"

"Thanks Jackie, but I'll admit that I was a bit scared of losing myself after moving into a robot body. There were so many things that could have gone wrong, but Dr. Wang did a great job analyzing and preventing issues. We worked together the whole time, and I really enjoyed it. I'm looking forward to more work with her and NASA in the future."

"That's great news Leah. Now let's get into your physical capabilities. Can you run, jump, climb, and swim?"

"Yes, I can run up to 30 mph. I can jump pretty high and climb quickly too. But I suck at swimming because I never had a swimming pool or beach nearby, so I need to learn how to swim."

"Fascinating! This leads into my next question: can you learn like a normal person, or can you be programmed like a computer?"

Leah laughed, "I was hoping to automatically know all martial arts and be the next Bruce Lee, but we realized that if I opted for programming integration, then I would not have true free will and be prone to cyberattacks, so I refused. However, I can speak any language I want! Since I need a voice box to speak, I can select any language and my thoughts automatically get translated and sounded out for me."

"That's convenient, makes traveling the world much easier for you. Now since you mentioned martial arts, and your family and friends are superheroes, do you have any combat abilities?"

"My combat abilities are classified, so I'm not allowed to talk about specifics. However, I am allowed to use my combat abilities for self-defense and during emergencies. I just can't use them for fun, so don't worry everyone, robots are not taking over the world today!"

Jackie laughed, "I'm glad you have a sense of humor, which is perfect for our next segment. I'm going to blitz you with silly questions collected from the internet involving humanoid robots. Most of them only require Yes or No answers, but you can elaborate if you wish. Are you ready?"

"Yeah, this should be fun!" Leah declared with enthusiasm.

"Okay, here we go! Do you need to brush your teeth?"

"No, but I like using mouthwash."

"Take a shower?"

"Yes."

"Wear clothes?"

"Yes! Oh my gosh!"

"Eat, drink, breathe?"

"No eating, but I do need water occasionally and I don't breathe."

"Plug yourself into a wall with electricity?"

"Hahaha, no I'm not a cellphone that needs constant charging."

"Can you make art?"

"I suck at art! I can only draw stick people."

"Can you play any musical instruments?"

"I like playing horns and drums in marching band."

"Do you play any sports?"

"I'm great at softball and tennis."

"Can you survive in space?"

"Supposedly, but I still want a protective suit just in case."

"Are you super smart?"

"Not really, but I am a fast reader."

"Can you kiss?"

"Yes."

"Fall in love?"

"Probably."

"Reproduce?"

"Aaaahh!!! No! I don't want robot babies!"

"Do you want to date or get married one day?"

"Totally! But it has to be someone who gets me and thinks I'm awesome!"

"That's the spirit, Leah! Never settle for anything less. Now I do have one last question, and it's a deep one, so here goes. Do you like being a robot?"

Leah paused for a moment, then she looked down nervously and explained, "I don't know. I'm happy to be alive and I know this was the best option. I've got cool features and I can interact with the world like a person, but it's scary. People might judge me, fear me, or think I'm weird. I might have trouble making new friends. I may not be allowed to do certain activities because I'm a robot. I also don't know if I'll become obsolete or live forever. I want to live, grow, and enjoy life with friends and family...I don't want to end up alone."

Jerry got out of his chair, knelt on one knee next to Leah's chair, and gave her a warm hug. Then he said, "Your mother and I will never abandon you. We have unique powers of belief that can probably make us ageless or immortal, so you don't have to worry about that."

Jackie stared at Jerry with her mouth open and the audience began a controversial debate about immortality. In history, people were obsessed with the fountain of youth and went on deadly expeditions to find it. Kings and emperors spent much of their gold trying to find or create immortality. For the general public today, having superpowers was already hard to swallow, but immortality seemed impossible and even taboo. People aren't meant to live forever, and if it was possible, then others may want that power...Jerry and Cynthia's power.

People began arguing and shouting as news reporters stormed the stage to demand answers. They wanted to know everything about Jerry and Cynthia's powers, seeing this as a major news headline. World leaders also spoke out, demanding a private audience with the newlyweds. Jackie and her team tried squashing the frenzied audience, but it was no use. Jerry and Cynthia made a quick decision, grabbed Leah's hand, and teleported away. Nobody knew where they went; their honeymoon location and activities were a secret.

Chapter 21:
HONEYMOON SPECIAL

"WHERE ARE WE?" Cynthia wondered.

"Are we lost?" Leah asked.

"No, we're not lost...I just can't remember the name of this place," Jerry murmured.

"Are you kidding me?" Cynthia blurted out with an annoyed tone.

"I'm sorry!" Jerry apologized, "I was under pressure with everyone rushing the stage and yelling. I just wanted to get us out of there quickly."

"We're standing on a giant red rock...is this Mars?" Leah joked.

"No," Jerry laughed, "We're in Australia, a landmark I saw online. It's the first thing that popped in my head when deciding where to go for our honeymoon."

"How come you never told me?" Cynthia interrogated Jerry.

"I had to keep it a secret from everyone. I didn't want people finding out and hunting us down for pictures and interviews," Jerry explained.

Cynthia calmed down and admitted, "It's a nice place to visit, never been here before and it's definitely on my bucket list."

"Great! I can't wait to see it all!" Leah exclaimed as she began running around different parts of the mysterious red rock.

In a national park in the center of Australia, they stood upon a famous monolith called Uluru. It looked like a small mountain, standing over a thousand feet tall with 5-6 miles of surface area. As Leah looked over the edge, she saw endless fields of grass with pockets of red soil. The sky was blue, and the air was fresh. There were no roads nor cities in sight; they truly were in the middle of nowhere.

Thankfully, Jerry and Cynthia had superpowers. They wanted to explore a few miles around this historic site without disturbing wildlife, so they took a minute to meditate. Jerry absorbed water from clouds in the sky and transformed into a water elemental, featuring an armor of thick, white, and blue water flowing all over his body. Cynthia created a vacuum of swirling air around herself and transformed into an air elemental, with white and gray-colored wind flowing around her. They each grabbed one of Leah's hands and took flight! Both their water and wind powers enveloped Leah like a protective barrier that carried her with them across the Australian landscape.

Leah was in awe of her parents and everything around her. They were flying about 30 feet above the ground. She excitedly pointed out various animals that were all new to her.

"There are so many different colored birds! Red, black, white, gray, green, blue, and yellow!"

"Look at the horses and camels! They're so big!"

"Is that a wild dog, or a wolf?"

"None," Jerry clarified, "That's a dingo!"

"Can I pet it?" Leah requested.

"You can try!" Jerry answered swiftly and flew Leah down closer to the ground.

Like a good mother, Cynthia anxiously told Jerry, "What if it's dangerous?"

"She'll be fine!" Jerry responded nonchalantly, "She's gotta learn somehow, right? We'll help her if needed."

Cynthia watched keenly as Leah slowly approached the dingo on foot. The dingo was light brown and white colored, lying low and observing Leah with distrust. Its ears perked up when Leah got within 20 feet, and it charged at her! It tried biting Leah multiple times, but her lightning reflexes kicked in and she dodged every attack. She was excited, treating this as a game to test her combat abilities. After multiple failed attacks, the dingo jumped backwards and began to growl.

Leah slowly knelt down on one knee and began begging the dingo to come to her, but it kept growling. Eventually, she remembered Jerry's early stories about interacting with fish in the ocean, so Leah began to sing a song.

Pretty doggie, come to me.
I will pet you, soft and free.
I promise not to hurt or touch,
I only want to play and watch.

Cynthia was worried it wouldn't work, but Jerry was confident and believed in his daughter, silently cheering her on. The dingo stopped growling and cautiously approached Leah. She closed her eyes and put all her faith and trust in the dingo. Seconds later, she felt a nose, then fur, and she opened her eyes to find the dingo nuzzling her hand. She smiled and enjoyed the moment, then began petting and talking to the dingo like a dog.

"Good boy! I love you so much!"

After more petting, she wanted to reward the dingo, so she pointed one her right pinky fingers into her hand left hand and squirted out water! The dingo began fervently licking the water out of her hand and wagging its tail. After it finished drinking, Leah gave the dingo a final hug and whispered, "Thank you doggie, it was nice to meet you." Then she gave it a kiss on the head and walked away. The dingo understood and scurried off.

Jerry and Cynthia picked Leah up and they continued flying toward the nearest city. Leah saw a red kangaroo and shouted, "Look at its muscles! It's so strong! Can we see it up-close?"

"No!" Cynthia immediately replied, "Do you know how powerful they are? Kangaroos can kick you with over 700 pounds of force!"

"Wow! That's amazing!" Leah resounded with surprise.

Cynthia wanted to explore more, but she felt tired from the wedding and wanted a nice hotel to check into, so she urged Jerry and Leah to hurry along. Jerry smiled and revealed, "Don't worry, I've got it all planned out. Close your eyes and I'll take the lead." Then he picked up Cynthia and held her in his arms like a superhero. He also told Leah to jump on his back and hold on tight.

Jerry formed a protective barrier around everyone, then he flew faster than the speed of sound! In less than a minute, they arrived at their destination; a 5-star hotel only a few miles away from Uluru. Cynthia opened her eyes and saw several buildings with solar panels on the roofs. She also saw beautiful green trees, a large swimming pool, and yellow umbrellas as tall as buildings!

Jerry brought everyone into the hotel lobby. The hotel staff were very kind and greeted Jerry, Cynthia, and Leah with great respect. They showed them to their two rooms: one for Leah and one for Jerry & Cynthia. Jerry & Cynthia's room had one king-size bed, a royal bathroom with a jacuzzi, and an outdoor covered wooden deck overlooking the landscape. Leah's room had two full-sized beds with a low-hanging decorative light, an oversized bathtub, and various oils and cosmetic products. Everyone enjoyed their rooms and soon fell asleep, including Leah who has a sleep function to give her mind a break and recharge her energy.

The next two days were spent exploring popular tourist sites in Australia. On the first day, they visited the Twelve Apostles, a collection of seven limestone stacks along the coast. The limestone stacks are giant rock formations that are over 100 feet tall. Jerry, Cynthia, and Leah flew on top of and explored each one, taking pictures and enjoying the sun and sea breeze.

Next, they visited the Wave Rock; a granite formation about 45 feet tall and 300 feet long that looks like the perfect wave for surfing. Cynthia took pictures and admired the Wave Rock like a normal tourist. Jerry and Leah, however, had a more fun idea. Jerry used his powers to create a magic ball and play *Catch* with Leah, rolling the ball into the Wave Rock like a ramp for increased difficulty and amusement.

On the second day, they visited the Three Sisters, a mountainous area with three famous peaks and numerous trees and wildlife. Jerry, Cynthia, and Leah enjoyed exploring the peaks, climbing trees, and interacting with animals and birds. There were also many tourists observing from afar. As a special treat, Jerry and Cynthia used their powers to give tourists a better view. They created a huge magical basket, tourists stepped into it, and they carried the tourists into the air and around the Three Sisters! The tourists were overjoyed; taking pictures and repeatedly thanking Jerry & Cynthia for the unique experience.

Lastly, they attended a tour of the Sydney Opera House. Starting from the outside, the opera house roofs (consisting of over 1 million ceramic tiles) are quite unique; they look like several white triangular sails are fused together and pointing in random directions. There are massive stairs, hundreds of feet wide, in front of the opera house; the stairs are so big that people walking on them look like ants in comparison. Inside the six concert halls, where famous performances regularly occur, there are enough seats for 5,800 guests! They have different types of lighting and sound speakers all over the ceilings, which are at various heights and shapes to create musical harmony. Jerry and Leah were dying to sing on stage and hear their voices echo throughout the concert hall, but Cynthia kept them under control.

While on vacation, Jerry, Cynthia, and Leah visited Salamanca Market multiple times to eat fresh food and mingle with citizens. Jerry & Cynthia enjoyed various hot meals, fruits, vegetables, desserts, and drinks all while Leah watched with bittersweet feelings. Not needing to eat or drink for survival was cool, but she missed the sensation of tasting different foods, drinks, seasonings, and flavors. One time while Jerry & Cynthia were eating, she decided to walk around the market alone and explore. Luckily, she met a curious young man named Jaxon. He had pale white skin, blonde hair, blue eyes, and wore jeans and a video game t-shirt. He recognized Leah from the televised wedding and interview.

"I know you, you're Leah! I can't believe you're here!"

"Yep, I'm here and I'm real, but I don't know you." Leah rebutted.

"Sorry about that, my name is Jaxon and I think you're incredible!"

"Really?" Leah admitted with surprise.

"Of course! I thought your interview on TV was so cool."

"Thanks, Jaxon, but tell me your favorite part so I know you actually watched it."

"My favorite part was when you stood up and yelled at the guy for telling you to cut yourself. He was a total jerk."

"I know right! Screw that guy!" Leah exclaimed, then she laughed at the memory, thinking how crazy it was to scream at a guy on live TV.

"I like your laugh," Jaxon admitted sincerely.

Leah blushed and replied, "I like your eyes...and your shirt too! Are you good at video games?"

Jaxon smiled and began talking about his favorite video games. Leah also spoke about her gaming experiences, and they seemed to get along quite well. Eventually, Jaxon revealed that he lives in America, but he's visiting his uncle and aunt in Australia for vacation. Leah became very excited and courageously asked Jaxon for his cellphone. He agreed and she gave him her contact information. They promised each other to keep in touch and hang out again soon. They both parted ways and went to go looking for their respective family members.

Leah felt happy; Jaxon was the first boy to have a meaningful conversation with her after she became a robot. Most people asked her lots of dumb questions about being a robot, but Jaxon was special because he treated her like a completely normal person.

When Leah returned to Jerry and Cynthia, they both looked very serious as if something was wrong. When Leah asked them, Jerry explained.

"Tomorrow, we have work to do. There's protesting happening between Chinese and Australian citizens at the Parliament House, the main government building for Australia."

Cynthia chimed in, "Rumor has it that tomorrow may get violent, so we want to be there and make sure nobody gets hurt."

"Yes! This will be my first hero mission!" Leah hollered.

However, Jerry and Cynthia looked at each other worriedly, then they each gave different excuses for Leah not to join them tomorrow.

"We're not citizens of Australia, so we have to be extra careful," Cynthia clarified.

"I wanted your first hero mission to be a small crime, something easy to manage, but protests with thousands of people can become dangerous very quickly." Jerry reasoned.

"So what? I'm a robot with combat abilities, I can handle this!" Leah begged.

Jerry and Cynthia knew Leah would not accept this easily, so they offered a compromise.

"How about you explore Australia alone? It'll be your first chance to have true independence and control over your life." Jerry tried persuading her.

"You can go wherever you want, and if you have any problems, you can contact us, and we'll come to you right away. We only ask that you stay away from the Parliament House protests." Cynthia pleaded.

Leah didn't like being excluded from the mission, but she remembered how kind Jaxon was and knew exactly what to do. She gave her parents a thumbs up and agreed not to attend the protests. But, if someone else wanted to go and she had to protect them, that would be different, right? She did not mention her thinking to her parents and contacted Jaxon to hangout tomorrow. Jaxon was delighted and stunned, not expecting a call from Leah so quickly. Leah was eager to see Jaxon again, and determined to attend the protests, one way or another.

Chapter 22:
RACIAL TENSION

"YOU PEOPLE ARE SPREADING DISEASES and viruses around the world!" Australians protested.

"We've done nothing wrong; we're vaccinated!" Chinese civilians retorted.

"Show us proof!"

"We don't have to! It's illegal to make us do that!"

"Who cares! You've got nothing to hide, right?" Australians questioned.

"We will not submit to your demands! We are not slaves or illegal immigrants; we have the same rights as you do!" Chinese civilians declared.

"You don't deserve any rights! You should be banished!"

"How dare you! We work harder than you do! We've earned our place here!"

"You'll never be one of us! Go back to your country!" Australians commanded.

"We'll fight everyone to stay here! This is our home too!"

A brave news reporter was standing up close to the protestors, capturing all the intense moments for television viewers. There were thousands of protestors arguing in front of the Parliament House, the main government building for Australia. They all held large signs with loud and rude messages; some supporting Australians and others supporting Chinese. Leah was at Jaxon's home, sitting on a nearby recliner chair and watching the conflict on TV.

Leah was excited because she knew Jerry and Cynthia were there and she wanted to see them on TV. She was also hoping for wild superhero action to occur, any excuse to go out and kick some butt. However, Jaxon was bored, sitting alone on a couch and looking at his cellphone. Eventually, he decided to speak up.

"I thought you called me to hang out and play video games, but you've been watching the news ever since you got here."

"Yeah, I'm sorry," Leah apologized, "I'm just really into this stuff. My parents are there too, so I hope something crazy happens."

"My uncle and aunt are there too, and I hope nothing happens."

"Wait, why are your uncle and aunt there? Are they protesting?" Leah asked.

"No, they're superheroes here in Australia."

"What? Why didn't you tell me earlier?"

"I thought you already knew...I figured that was the only reason you befriended me." Jaxon admitted with disappointment.

"No, of course not! I really like you!"

"You do?" Jaxon said with surprise.

"Yeah!" Leah excitedly replied and turned off the TV. Then she stood up from the recliner chair and sat down next to Jaxon on the couch.

Jaxon was speechless, he felt nervous with Leah next to him...he didn't have much experience with girls. Leah smiled, knowing she caught him off-guard. She liked being in charge and led the conversation.

"So, tell me about your uncle and aunt."

"Uncle Marqui teaches people how to do watersports like wakeboarding. Aunt Nicole is a schoolteacher. They don't like using their powers, but sometimes the government asks them for help." Jaxon explained.

"Why don't they like using their powers?"

"They just want to live normal lives. They don't want the pressure and high expectations of being superheroes. My uncle's also a bit grumpy and thinks most people are dumb and not worth fighting for. But he's a good guy, so he'll help occasionally, especially if Nicole asks him to."

Leah paused for a moment to think. She couldn't understand why people wouldn't want powers. Leah was dying to be a superhero, and Jerry loved it! Cynthia was a bit hesitant at first, but even she and all of Jerry's friends eventually began to enjoy it and are proud of their work as heroes.

Noticing that Leah was daydreaming, Jaxon nudged her, "So you want to play a video game?"

"Sure, let's do it!"

Leah turned on the TV, then she purposely picked up a nearby magazine and began flipping through the pages to avoid the news of the protest on TV. She wanted to make a good impression and enjoy spending time with Jaxon instead of obsessing over superhero stuff. While Jaxon was pulling out game controllers and setting everything up, however, he noticed a battle happening on the news!

"My uncle and aunt are fighting against a Chinese woman and Jerry!"

"What? Why?"

"I don't know, but we have to help them!" Jaxon proclaimed.

"How? You don't have superpowers!" Leah blurted out.

"But you do! Isn't this what you wanted?"

"At the beginning, yeah, but then you made me feel guilty about it. You also made me realize that I need a break from superhero stuff."

"Forget all that!" Jaxon anxiously exclaimed, "Our family members are in trouble! Please help!"

Leah grinned, "Well, if you put it that way, let's go!"

Leah and Jaxon grabbed their stuff and sprinted out the door, determined to help their families at the protest.

***

Marqui, a short blonde-haired man wearing cargo shorts but shirtless with six-pack abs, was throwing numerous magical hammers at Jerry. Jing, a Chinese woman standing behind Jerry, was watching as he deflected the hammers harmlessly into the sky with his hands. Jing became irritated and interrogated Jerry.

"Why are you helping me? You're not Chinese!"

"It doesn't matter what I am! I'm helping you because everyone deserves equal treatment!" Jerry answered.

"I don't need your help! I can fight on my own!"

"Why are you fighting? Why not try negotiating for equality?"

"You don't think I tried that?" Jing exclaimed, "These pompous politicians won't listen to our people! They only care about money!"

"There has to be a better way than this!" Jerry countered.

"No! Only by making noise and forcing people to care can we actually succeed. They won't listen until their Parliament House crumbles!"

Jerry wanted to continue arguing, but someone interfered. Nicole, a skinny blonde-haired woman, created a 15-foot long pole of chalk and launched it at Jing's back! Jing flexed her back muscles, causing the chalk to explode upon impact. The explosion created a cloud of chalk that covered Jing and Jerry, blocking their vision and burning their skin. Jerry screamed, releasing a burst of energy and wind that dispersed the chalk cloud.

When the chalk cloud disappeared, however, Marqui was already charging at Jerry with a huge two-handed magic hammer! He slammed his hammer into Jerry and sent him flying hundreds of feet into the air! Jerry barely managed to defend himself, putting up a blue energy shield that prevented himself from being harmed, but knocking him that far away certainly annoyed him. Jerry was trying to stop the fighting and felt like everyone was making things worse.

Jing became angry and used her super-strength to smash the ground and cause an earthquake! Marqui threw his hammer at Jing during the earthquake to try and stop her, but it bounced off her rubber-like body and shot back at Marqui! Marqui put his arms up for protection and took the hammer hit head-on; it knocked him to the ground and his arms were bloody and severely bruised. The earthquake caused the building to shake and people inside were panicking. Some people were running out of the building while others were scared and hiding under furniture.

Meanwhile, thousands of Australian and Chinese protestors were fighting each other; yelling, punching, wrestling, breaking signs, throwing objects, and pushing against police officers who had large riot shields. Cynthia was on damage-control duty and using her powers in various ways. She was electrocuting protestors, healing the wounded, and holding the Parliament House molecules together to keep the building from collapsing and killing everyone. Cynthia also observed the fighting closely, taking notes in her mind in case she had to fight later.

Finally, Leah and Jaxon arrived at the scene. Jaxon ran to Nicole, and they tried helping people who were hurt or fallen on the ground due to the earthquake. Jerry zoomed into the Parliament House to save and evacuate victims. Leah rushed to Cynthia and asked how she could help. Cynthia was upset that Leah disobeyed her and came to the protest, but she was also relieved. She informed Leah about the situation, including everyone's powers, strengths, and weaknesses.

Marqui, however, was furious! He stood up, concentrated his powers, and created dozens of small magical hammers floating around Jing. He controlled the hammers with his mind and began pummeling her like a pinata. Jing crouched down to protect herself. Even though she could make attacks bounce off her rubber-like body, it still required energy and focus. Marqui had so many hammers hitting her simultaneously that she couldn't move. Marqui vented and argued with Jing during the assault.

"You think you can do whatever you want? There are laws for a reason!"

"Your laws have failed! The Chinese live in fear!" Jing retorted.

"You don't care about Chinese rights and equality; you only want chaos!"

"That's not true!"

"You want to be right! You want to prove you're better than others!" Marqui proclaimed as he continued attacking Jing with endless magical hammers.

"No!"

"You're an idiot! You're wasting everyone's time and tax dollars! Your actions are pointless!"

"Never! Raaaaaaahh!!!!" Jing roared and charged through the hammers! She suffered damage and bled, but she made it out and punched Marqui as hard as she could. Before hitting Marqui, Nicole launched a chalk pike at Jing's face, cutting and blinding her, causing Jing's attack to hit Marqui on the shoulder instead of his chest. With Jing's super strength, she probably would have killed Marqui with a chest hit, but she instead dislocated Marqui's shoulder and made his body spin several times in the air before hitting the ground. Marqui was prone, groaning in pain and unable to fight; Nicole screamed for someone to help him.

Everyone else was busy except Leah, so it was her turn to step up. She yelled at Jing for attention, who was enraged and turned to fight Leah. Leah paid close attention and dodged all her attacks. Jing had super strength, but she was blinded by chalk and too slow to hit Leah. Leah had a rhythm, evading attacks like a dancer. Thanks to Cynthia's previous information, Leah knew exactly how to stop Jing and tried warning her several times. Jing refused to listen and continued throwing haymakers, wildly powerful punches with minor shockwaves.

Leah soon gave up on diplomacy and punched Jing in the throat. Normally her attack would bounce off Jing's rubber-like body, but Leah was able to use her power to go through objects and punch Jing under her skin! Jing immediately began choking and fell down gasping for air. She tried to speak but it was impossible to understand her. Cynthia ran up to Jing, placed her hand on Jing's forehead, and eased her pain, causing her to fall asleep. Jing was alive, but no longer a threat. The chaos ended, the protest was over, and everyone survived. Police were about to arrest Jing, but Jerry interfered.

"This event happened because her people's needs were ignored. She fought for their rights and put herself in danger."

"What about the destruction of the Parliament House? What about everyone who was injured? That woman must be brought to justice!" The police reasoned.

"What if we fix the building and cure the wounded right now, then will you pardon her?" Jerry requested.

"Impossible!" The Police declared.

Cynthia raised her hands, concentrated her power, and began pulling all the molecules of the Parliament House back together. Chunks of cement, wood, and other parts of the building slowly floated into place. In less than a minute, the government building was 100% rebuilt and looked cleaner than before. Then Jerry released waves of pure white energy over everyone in the area. Cuts & bruises disappeared, broken bones mended, and everyone's injuries were fully healed.

People were shocked and in awe. Had they not seen and experienced the miracle themselves; they would have never believed it. The Parliament House and everyone around it seemed healthy and in perfect shape as if nothing bad had ever happened. Politicians were speechless, but also secretly angry, feeling like the Believers stole the spotlight.

Nicole hugged Jaxon, thanking him for bringing Leah and her friends to help stop the protest. Cynthia hugged Leah, thanking her for stopping Jing and saving everyone. Jing soon woke up confused, but ready to fight again. However, Jerry put his hand on Jing's shoulder, looked at the politicians, and proposed, "Can we discuss this matter safely and calmly inside the Parliament House? Let's find a solution that works for everyone."

The politicians wanted to immediately say *No* and arrest Jing, but the news cameras were rolling and many onlookers had their cellphones posting the event live on social media. Wanting to maintain good public relations and get re-elected in the future, the politicians reluctantly agreed and spent hours inside the Parliament House resolving the issue. During the political event, Marqui and Jerry agreed to keep watch and prevent further problems. By the end of it, politicians agreed to pass legislation making it illegal to discriminate against Chinese civilians in Australia.

The next day, Jerry, Cynthia, Leah, Jaxon, Nicole, and Marqui ate brunch together and bonded over their shared experiences. Eventually, Jerry & Cynthia decided to end their honeymoon and return to America. Before leaving, however, everyone said their goodbyes and Marqui shook Jerry's hand.

"I don't like what you did and how you did it, but it all worked out." Marqui admitted.

"I'm sorry about interfering, but I couldn't sit back and watch." Jerry rebutted.

"Yeah well, don't do it again." Marqui added.

"Fair enough but give us a call in the future if you ever need help." Jerry offered.

"I won't." Marqui responded stubbornly.

Nicole laughed and chimed in, "My husband's kidding and we'd love to see you all again in the future, especially if you can bring Jaxon with you. He also lives in Miami, Florida, and I'm sure he'll keep in touch with Leah and enjoy any excuse to visit us again. Thanks for all your help and have a safe trip back home."

Leah and Jaxon gave each other a hug and smiled. Cynthia thanked them all and Jerry waved goodbye, then he teleported with his family back home.

Chapter 23:
HURRICANE MAYHEM

"A HURRICANE HAS DEVASTATED PUERTO RICO."

"The country is now in shambles!"

"Residents' homes are destroyed, literally reduced to rubble."

"They have no electricity and clean water is scarce."

"The U.S. President has announced his plans to send aid immediately."

"How long will it take Puerto Rico to recover from this crisis?"

"I'd say a minimum of 2 months for cleanup and basic functionality, but it could take years to restore Puerto Rico to its former glory."

"Thank you for your input, we'll be back shortly with more news and updates about Puerto Rico."

Jerry and Cynthia were sitting together on the couch watching the news on TV. It's been one year since their honeymoon in Australia. Jerry chose to slowdown his hero work, only helping with dire emergencies, so he could focus more on his family. Leah had to complete space missions for NASA, so Jerry often tagged along or observed to ensure her safety. She also worked with Jaxon to complete online high school courses and prepare for college in the future. Most importantly, Cynthia was working as a full-time nurse while studying to become a doctor. Cynthia and Leah were constantly busy, so Jerry had to cook dinners, clean the house, do laundry, and accomplish most domestic tasks on his own. Jerry never complained because he enjoyed being a super dad/husband and taking care of his family.

After they saw the news on TV, however, both of their phones rang. The government requested their help with recovery efforts in Puerto Rico. The government also informed them that they must travel via airplane to meet all humanitarian workers and discuss the plan of action. Cynthia was eager to attend because she needed volunteer hours and this event would allow her to practice her skills as a nurse and future doctor.

Before leaving, they reviewed all house rules with Leah. They asked her to take a break from NASA work while they were gone. They also wanted her to focus on her online high school courses. Lastly, they encouraged her to have fun and enjoy time with Jaxon. They reminisced about their high school days being the best time of their lives and wanted the same thing for Leah. Leah gave her parents a hug, wished them good luck, and they soon left for the airport.

When Jerry and Cynthia arrived, they met a familiar face...Agent X. They shook hands and boarded the airplane with several government personnel and humanitarian workers. The plane was large and spacious. The business class seating was very comfortable, providing plenty of leg space and a generous area between seats for personal items. There were TVs displaying images and videos of Puerto Rico, showing the extensive damage from the hurricane. During the flight, Agent X gave a general speech to everyone about work and expectations in Puerto Rico, then he approached groups of individuals with detailed instructions. Each group received a specialized document, including maps of work areas, facilities, goals/tasks, warnings/dangers, etc.

Since Jerry & Cynthia have superpowers, Agent X asked questions and discussed the best ways to utilize them. Jerry agreed to let Cynthia care for the wounded while he completed rescue and restoration activities. Since they can both fly and teleport, they will be working all over Puerto Rico and have hand-held radios for Agent X and other government personnel to coordinate with them.

When they finally arrived in Puerto Rico, they couldn't believe what they saw...it was far worse than any prior pictures, videos, or information provided. It looked like the aftermath of a war.

Torrential rain caused mudslides that destroyed everything in their path. Roads were broken and impassable due to fallen trees, drowned cars, and entire homes floating or smashed to pieces. There was so much debris that even boats couldn't make it through. All remaining homes were heavily damaged and flooded with water. Thousands of people died and many more were injured or missing. The survivors were suffering, in desperate need of food, water, electricity, and medical assistance.

All government personnel and humanitarian workers followed the plan and began working in their assigned areas. Cynthia began working with fellow doctors and nurses to assess the health of nearby survivors by organizing them into three categories: safe, injured, or dying. Cynthia knew Puerto Rico had a population of over 3 million people, so she conserved her energy and only used her powers to save dying patients. She also worked alongside doctors and nurses to assist and learn as they treated injured people using normal medical procedures.

Jerry's job was more complicated and spanned the entire island. His first and most vital task was to locate all the injured and dying people who were missing. Jerry sat on the ground and began meditating. After a few moments, thousands of red energy strings shot out from Jerry and spread all over the island. Jerry had successfully located every single injured and dying person who was missing and was now connected to them with his energy. He could sense their injuries and state of mind, receiving an overload of information.

Jerry knew there were too many people to rescue individually, and the amount of time needed may cause many of them to die or worsen their condition. Time was the enemy, but Jerry had an ambitious plan to save them all at once. He walked out into a large open space, then he summoned most of his energy and expended it all at once! The red strings vibrated with distortion, then suddenly, all the missing injured and dying victims appeared around him! He successfully teleported them all, thousands of victims! They were all confused and groaning in pain, but some of them had realized the miracle that occurred. The ones who could began shouting for help.

Cynthia and the medical staff rushed over and couldn't believe it. Jerry stood in the middle of them all, weary and exhausted. He gave a thumbs up and fell unconscious. Cynthia and the medical staff worked tirelessly for the next 12 hours, healing as many people as they could, all while Jerry slept. After 12 hours, Jerry woke up refreshed and ready to work. Cynthia gave him a kiss and took a rest, then Jerry reported to Agent X for a mission update.

"Jerry, I heard you were sleeping on the job!"

"Yeah, go ahead, make all the jokes you want."

"I'm just messing with ya. You did a great job bringing all those people to our main encampment, saved us a lot of time!" Agent X reassured him.

"Thanks," Jerry nodded, "Now tell me what's next."

"The easy part is you flying around the island using your powers to help restore fallen buildings. Focus on homes, schools, hospitals, gas stations, grocery stores, power plants, water treatment facilities, anything you think is essential. Speak Spanish with the locals and they'll help you too."

"I can do that," Jerry agreed, "Anything else I need to know?"

Agent X looked around, making sure nobody else could hear their conversation, then he leaned close to Jerry and whispered, "What if I told you there might be another hurricane coming?"

Jerry felt alarmed and continued their conversation telepathically, "Are you serious?"

"Yep, talk about bad luck, right? Our meteorologists are saying that a big storm is brewing and heading here. It'll gain strength along the way and hit in a few days."

"Is there a chance it might turn away?" Jerry asked.

"Maybe, but it would be a real shame if all the work we're doing here was a waste of time. Can you stop the storm from hitting us?

"What? Me? How?"

"Come on Jerry, you got superpowers, this should be easy for you."

Jerry hesitated, then he made an excuse and left to help rebuild Puerto Rico. While Cynthia continued working with nurses and doctors to heal people, Jerry traveled around the island using his powers to restore buildings. He spoke with several citizens to learn about the buildings, looked at pictures on the internet, and did his best. People were amazed by his powers, staring in awe as Jerry pulled cement, wood, dirt, steel, leaves, rocks, and debris from the surrounding areas to put buildings back together. These different elements floated in the air, then magically combined together in the shape and form of the original buildings. Some buildings appeared the same or better than before, but others came out looking funky and citizens laughed or seemed confused. Regardless, Jerry did the best he could, and people cheered him on, knowing that his work was a miracle and saved them tons of time, energy, money, and resources.

Days passed as Jerry worked in Puerto Rico. He learned a lot about the people and their culture. He felt happy when families smiled and hugged him, even offering small rewards for his hard work. He refused every reward and said, "Thank you for trusting me to help you." Jerry's Spanish was mediocre, but people understood and appreciated him greatly, many considering him a god or angel sent to help them. Jerry felt very guilty and uneasy about that, always believing he was just like everyone else, but deep down, he knew the truth. He knew the next hurricane was coming soon, and he had various thoughts in his mind.

Can I really let these people die? All the work we've done to restore their country would be pointless if another hurricane destroyed it. Even though I helped restore many buildings, Puerto Rico is still lacking food, water, and electricity. Another hurricane would devastate them, setting them back for years! They may never recover because it would cost billions or trillions of dollars! But truthfully, I'm more worried about God and my place in the world. God gave me these powers for a reason, but I don't think it was to act as God. Hurricanes are part of nature and occur regularly around the world, along with tsunamis, earthquakes, etc. If I save Puerto Rico, should I save every country? What's the right path? I don't want to overstep or abuse my powers.

***

It was time to evacuate the island due to the arrival of the 2nd hurricane. It was an unprecedented event to have two hurricanes hit back-to-back in such a short time. Jerry had spoken with Cynthia about his concerns and asked her to leave with everyone else. There was lots of paperwork to complete based on their work in Puerto

Rico, none of which Cynthia had ever done before, so Jerry wanted her to learn all about it. Cynthia knew this was an excuse to get her out of danger, but she complied knowing that Jerry wanted to handle this hurricane situation alone. She understood that this was not a physical danger for Jerry, but more of a mental and philosophical danger. Jerry needed to decide his place in the world as a hero, how far he was willing to go with his powers, and what was considered acceptable or not in the eyes of God.

All government personnel and humanitarian workers left, including Cynthia. A few citizens of Puerto Rico escaped, but many foolishly stayed to protect their land and prayed the storm would turn away. Jerry heard the citizens' prayers with his super hearing as he stood upon a rock at the edge of the island, waiting for the storm to hit. He spent the entire time praying to God, asking for understanding and forgiveness for whatever decision he chose. Jerry could feel the winds increasing, the animals hiding, the people crying, even the island shuttering in fear.

Jerry felt tension in his chest, pain in his heart and soul. He knew what he wanted to do, but needed reassurance, a sign that it was the right thing to do. In his moment of internal struggle, a lightning bolt struck him! His body jolted in pain; the electricity shot through his body and affected him greatly. He felt fried, but also emboldened. He knew that he only survived because of his powers; normal citizens would not be so lucky. Jerry now understood that he was here for a reason. He cannot be expected to save every country from every natural disaster. He cannot act as a robot and patrol the world 24/7 to prevent every death. But he was here now, in the right place and time, to take action and save lives. It would be an evil act to stand by and watch people die.

He began floating in the sky, yelling in rage as he summoned great power! Blue beams of light shot out everywhere, like a spiderweb of pure energy entangling the entire hurricane. He soon gained complete control of the hurricane and proceeded to guide it on a new path. He slowly pushed it along the upper coast of Puerto Rico, then forced it to make a hard turn north to the Sargasso Sea. He also flew into the sky and followed it for a few hours. He used his energy to slowly disrupt the hurricane inside and out, until it weakened and dispersed.

With the hurricane's last breath, Jerry heard a familiar female voice, "I'll be back, Jerry, take care." It was a voice from his past...Darci, a female supervillain who had worked with Sanchez. Could she still be alive in spirit, despite not having a physical body? She had the powers of fog and wind, but Von killed her during the Sanchez war, so maybe she transformed herself into wind before death. Jerry thought about this for a while as he flew back home to Cynthia and Leah.

Chapter 24:
ASTEROIDS

"JERRY! HOW'S EVERYTHING GOING?"

"Life is good, Von, no complaints here. How about you?"

"Other than kicking criminals' butts, a lot has happened since last time we spoke."

"Oh yeah? What's new?" Jerry asked.

"Well, I finally took Mr. Hamel's advice and decided to start a family, so I proposed to Alina."

"That's huge! Congrats, Von!"

"Thanks, Jerry. I wanted to tell you first because I really appreciate everything you've done for me. We've been through a lot together and I think I'm a better person for it."

"No worries bro, the feeling is mutual, you've helped me a lot too." Jerry admitted.

"Anyway, I gotta go call everyone else and let them know the big news. But we gotta get everyone together and celebrate soon." Von suggested.

"Absolutely! Can't wait to see you. Good luck and catch ya later."

"Thanks, Jerry. Peace!"

The phone call ended, and Jerry began to daydream. He was so proud of Von for overcoming all the challenges and dark times in his life. He was truly scared of Von losing himself after his father, Chief Grimes, died in the Sanchez war. Thankfully, Alina and all his friends helped him. Von fortified his mind, improved his combat abilities, and helped save the world. Now he's getting married and starting a family...what a success story.

Jerry also thought about his own life. He grew up completely different from everyone else, barely able to speak and struggling in school, all while learning how to manage his superpowers. He feared hurting himself and others, hiding his powers from the world, until great friends found him and helped. His family stepped up too, and Jerry was able to turn his life around. He became a global superhero, saved the world several times, got married, bought a home, and now lives happily with his wife and daughter. He felt like the luckiest guy in the world and couldn't ask for anything else.

Jerry was home alone because Cynthia was studying at the university and Leah was hanging out at Jaxon's family home. Jerry had just finished doing housework and was ready to sit down and relax. The moment Jerry sat on his favorite recliner chair, his phone started blaring like a siren and he pulled it out of his pocket...it was Agent X.

"Jerry! There's an asteroid crashing into Earth in less than 5 minutes!"

"What! How?"

"A random black hole opened up in space and an asteroid came through! It's the same size as the one that wiped out the dinosaurs!" Agent X hastily explained.

"Don't you guys have secret laser weapons or nukes to destroy it?"

"Yes, but there's not enough time! Everything we've got will take at least 10 minutes and we'll all be dead by then! You're our only hope! Please help!" Agent X pleaded.

"Got it. What's the best strategy here?" Jerry asked.

"Blow it up! Do whatever it takes! But you only get once chance, so don't hold back!" Agent X warned.

Jerry closed his phone and ran outside his house into the street. He looked up into the sky and saw the asteroid, clear as day, making its way towards Earth. There were a few people outside staring at the sky, wondering what was going on. They weren't panicking, they were struck with awe, thinking it was a beautiful sight and unaware of the imminent danger.

Jerry had never dealt with anything of this magnitude before, so he took time to think and prepare. Once he came up with a plan, he hit the red PANIC button on his phone and wrote a text message to all Believers around the world saying, "Look to the sky and wait for my signal, then stop whatever comes next."

Jerry knew that he needed far more energy than his own, so he concentrated and summoned fire and electricity into the center of his body, creating a new cyborg armor. His armor was metallic gray for defense, but thicker than usual and covered him head to toe. It was a better version of the spacesuit he wore when traveling in outer space for his NASA mission. He also had a lightning bolt on his chest with fire swirling around it.

Jerry walked over to the nearest electric utility pole, then he shot black cables from his cyborg suit upward to the top of the electric utility pole. His cables connected to the power lines above and he began rapidly absorbing electricity into his body. Jerry was draining the entire city power grid into himself, storing as much energy as possible. Jerry felt like a ticking time bomb, focusing all his will on containing the overwhelming energy surging into his body so it wouldn't explode prematurely.

People began freaking out as the power grid flickered and the asteroid grew bigger and closer to Earth. Jerry stared at the asteroid above and estimated that it was only a minute from impact. He was out of time and hoped he had enough energy to accomplish the task.

Jerry disconnected his black cables from the electric utility pole and bolted upward at the speed of light, charging head-on toward the asteroid. Within seconds, Jerry was high in the sky, above the earth at the edge of the atmosphere, inches away from the asteroid. It was at least the size of a country; a massive black rock that could easily wipe out most life on Earth. Jerry could also feel unnatural negative energy emitting from the asteroid, the same darkness that attacked the sun and possessed Sanchez in the past.

Upon making physical contact with the asteroid, Jerry phased through it! His body effortlessly glided into the center of the asteroid and *BOOM!* The world witnessed a massive explosion in the sky as the asteroid burst into millions of pieces. For everyone else, this event occurred in the blink of an eye, but it all happened for Jerry in slow-motion.

Moving at the speed of light altered Jerry's senses, allowing him to see and feel the world differently than normal. When he approached the asteroid, he could feel the overwhelming dark energy and decided to use it as a catalyst. He used his phasing ability to reach the center of the asteroid, then he simultaneously released both the stored electricity and his own fire energy. All this energy collided with the negative energy of the asteroid and caused a chain reaction of explosions. Jerry could see every point of contact bursting like fireworks all at once.

In Jerry's eyes, it was both beautiful and horrifying. He now realized how much power he had, more than any living creature should have. He literally held the power of life and death. Jerry chose to save the world, all by himself, as if he was a god. He made a decision that would forever alter history. What if humanity was supposed to be killed, like a reset button for the planet? Isn't that the same thing that happened to the dinosaurs? Would God, fate, and/or the universe allow humanity to live after this? Or is this the beginning of a bleak future? Should Jerry continue to exercise so much power? Lastly, was this asteroid targeting the earth, or Jerry?

All the thoughts above plagued Jerry's mind as the asteroid exploded all around him. His cyborg armor protected him from physical harm, but his senses were completely overwhelmed. His eyes were blinded, and his super-hearing caused booming sounds of the exploding asteroid to echo in his head and drown out everything else. He felt like he was stuck in a mental void, unable to react or do anything.

Jerry lost control and fell down to Earth. He crash-landed onto an open field in the middle of nowhere. His body hit the ground like a cannonball and made a giant crater. His armor protected him from the fall, but it now faded away and he was back to his normal self. He couldn't see or hear anything, but he felt his body go limp and relax. The grass and dirt caressed his body and acted like a bed; he finally had a moment of peace.

Jerry reminisced about all the times he'd been stuck in a crater. Every time had been painful, often during a battle where he was losing to an enemy. But this time was different...he felt calm and blissful. He saved the world and felt like he was being rewarded. Nature's soothing warmth surged through him, revitalizing him, making him feel whole again. He rested there for a long time, regenerating his energy, and allowing his mind & body to reset.

***

While Jerry was missing in action, Believers from around the world responded to the aftermath of the asteroid. When Jerry made the asteroid explode, the world's governments thought that the remaining small rocks would burn up in the atmosphere. However, the asteroid was infused with dark energy that protected the smaller rocks. Various Believers did the best they could to stop or divert the falling rocks, using an array of superpowers like wind, ice, telekinesis, energy blasts, gravity, barriers, hammers, fists, webs, etc. However, there were millions of small rocks traveling at about 700 MPH...causing the deaths of thousands of innocent people and millions of dollars in property damage.

When the barrage of rocks ended, everyone thought the crisis was over. Citizens walked outside to take pictures and post on social media. News vehicles went out in droves to cover the disaster story. Governments and hospitals sent out emergency services to assist the public.

Unfortunately, the event was far from over as all the small rocks from the asteroid began vibrating, rolling around, and merging into larger rocks. People watched with amazement, completely unaware of the danger to come. Soon the rocks transformed into sizable stone monsters, about 5 feet tall and wide, and began attacking everything in sight. They rolled and jumped everywhere, crashing through cars and buildings like wrecking balls. Citizens were terrified and running for their lives; there was nowhere safe to hide since the monsters were destroying everything. They had no faces and no emotion, causing mass destruction, injuries, and deaths everywhere without hesitation or remorse.

Believers around the world fought against these monsters with great difficulty. Nicole's chalk powers were ineffective as the rock monsters could not be burned nor blinded (since they had no eyes). Marqui used his hammer powers to crush the monsters into small rocks, but the rocks would slowly reforge back into large monsters again. Mega Fist produced similar results, pounding monsters into small rocks with his huge fists, only to see them form back into monsters too quickly. Blake and Jing were able to tackle and hold rock monsters, even smashing them into each other, but they were unable to destroy them. Mr. Cream successfully froze numerous monsters with ice, but they always managed to break the ice and escape after a few minutes. Mr. Miller was able to grab individual monsters, with his fiery hands, and melt them down into lava! The monsters would still reforge themselves, but at a much slower rate, allowing him to protect his home and neighbors.

Leah and Jaxon were hanging out together when they received the panic alert signal. Leah immediately rushed out to the streets to help civilians. Jaxon followed her, against her wishes, and watched as she took down rock monsters with her *classified* combat abilities. She would dash through multiple monsters, using her phasing ability to reach into them and release a burst of energy to make them explode from the inside.

Leah's attacks temporarily disabled the monsters, which gave Jaxon enough time to help victims get out of danger. However, one monster slipped past Leah and charged at Jaxon! She tried to stop it, but other monsters attacked and distracted her. Jaxon got so scared that he turned away from the monster and accidentally farted, releasing a violent burst of fire that blasted the monster away! Jaxon was a Believer! Leah was shocked. Jaxon always wanted to be a superhero like Leah, but he was embarrassed about his power.

"Really? Atomic farts? Why, God, why?" Jaxon asked.

Leah laughed, "I think it's my fault."

"How?"

"Well, I always wanted you to have powers and fight alongside me. But I also thought it would be funny if you had fart powers, so I thought about it all the time while with you. It was my secret joke that made me laugh, but I never thought it would actually come true." Leah explained.

"Are you kidding me? You gotta help me fix this! What if I fart in my sleep? I might burn the house down!"

Leah started dying of laughter. Jaxon wanted to stay mad, but he thought she was super cute and funny, so he also started laughing too. "I guess fire farts are better than no powers at all." Jaxon conceded.

Leah agreed, and they continued fighting rock monsters...together.

***

Von initially helped the police fight rock monsters with guns, but that wasn't very effective. Eventually, Von sensed the dark energy inside the monsters and began feeding on it, just as he did in the Sanchez war. Within minutes, Von drained all negative energy from rock monsters in the vicinity and gained immense power. After being drained, the monsters fell apart into useless rocks. Von soon transformed into pure darkness and closed his eyes to concentrate. With his close connection to the darkness, Von could pinpoint the location of every single monster like a *GPS* tracker.

Von perfectly focused his power, then he disappeared in the blink of an eye. He zoomed all throughout America at the speed of light. He bounced off rock monsters like a pinball, instantly draining their energy upon contact and fueling his own power. Von felt like a god as he destroyed most of the rock monsters in the country within minutes. He also continued into Central America, enjoying the adrenaline rush of decimating his enemies.

When Von ran out of rock monsters to drain nearby, however, he felt his own energy fading fast. He wanted to help more countries but didn't want to risk running out of energy in foreign territory, so he used everything he had to return to Miami. He barely made it to Alina's workplace, her therapy office. Luckily, her office had not been attacked and she was reading notes in preparation for an upcoming therapy session. When Von arrived, he collapsed in front of her, and she immediately tried to help him. She used her powers to scan his mind and body for injuries and information. Von was alive and safe, but he needed to rest.

Alina had received the panic alert on her phone just like all the other Believers, but she ignored it because she works as a full-time therapist. She also thought it was something the Believers could handle on their own, but she was wrong. After scanning Von's memories and watching his battles against the rock monsters, she realized that their connection to the darkness was extremely vital. These rock monsters aren't living creatures, they are simply objects being manipulated by dark energy. Whenever Von drained the monsters of their dark energy, they became useless rocks. What if Alina could use her powers to cut off or disrupt their connection to the darkness?

Cynthia was engaged in epic battles across the world. She realized that America had the most Believers to defend it, but other nations had far less Believers and desperately needed her help. Cynthia used her molecular powers to break down rock monsters permanently, but there were simply too many for her to handle alone. Alina contacted her with a possible solution.

"Cynthia! Where are you? I need your help!"

"Sorry Alina, I've been all over the place! There are so many monsters attacking all continents!"

"What if I told you I found a way to beat them all at once?"

"That would be amazing!" Cynthia exclaimed, "This feels like an endless battle right now. Tell me what to do."

"Pick me up and take me to NASA."

"You got it Alina! Be there soon."

Cynthia spent a few minutes wrapping things up in Africa, then she teleported to Alina and found Leah with her too. Cynthia was pleasantly surprised and gave her daughter a hug, then she wondered, "What happened to Jaxon?"

"He overused his new fart powers and exhausted himself, so I sent him home to rest."

"Sounds good to me," Cynthia agreed, "One less person to worry about.

"Wait, you're not curious about Jaxon's fart powers?" Leah asked, trying to hold her laughter.

"Oh, I'm very curious! I'm sure it'll be a ridiculous story, but let's save the world first." Cynthia suggested.

"By the way, I'm glad you're here Leah. We can use your help at NASA since you work there." Alina reasoned.

"Of course! I can't wait to takedown more rock monsters!" Leah excitedly replied.

"How are we doing that exactly?" Cynthia questioned.

"I'll explain later." Alina answered.

"Okay, let's go!"

Cynthia teleported to NASA with Leah and Alina. They appeared right in Dr. Wang's office, but she was hyper-focused and didn't even notice them. Dr. Wang was having a very important phone conversation with the President and White House staff. She was providing an update on how the black hole event occurred and any data they had about the rock monsters. Even though the monsters were defeated in America, the President wanted all available information to help allied countries and ways to prevent this disaster from happening again in the future. When she finished the conversation and hung up the phone, she looked up and was very relieved to see the girls.

"Oh, thank God you're here! Tell me you have good news." Dr. Wang pleaded.

"I think we can stop all the rock monsters around the world, but we need your NASA satellites." Alina declared.

"How would that help?" Dr. Wang asked with skepticism.

"During the Sanchez war, I learned how to block out negative energy and kept it from affecting my friends. I also analyzed Von's mind and learned how he drained enemies of their dark energy. I think I can alter my power and broadcast it around the world with NASA satellites to remove the negative energy from all remaining rock monsters." Alina expounded.

"Have you tested your power against these monsters?" Dr. Wang probed.

"Umm..." Alina hesitated.

"And even if your power does work, how can you send it through satellites?" Dr. Wang interrogated further.

Alina didn't have the right answers and Dr. Wang wanted to continue arguing, but Leah chimed in, "I lived inside a cellphone and computer for a long time! I learned how to fuse my powers with technology and manipulated multiple devices, I can help!"

"That's perfect Leah! I believe in you, and Dr. Wang doesn't have any better ideas, right? If this works, I'm sure someone will get big praise or a promotion." Cynthia negotiated with a smile, knowing Dr. Wang really had no better options.

Everyone stared at Dr. Wang until she finally conceded, "Fine! For the record, I think this will never work, but let's try and hope for the best. Follow me."

They all walked into the control room, where countless computers and personnel were all working frantically. The world was under siege by stone monsters and NASA was expected to do something about it since the event began in space. Dr. Wang sat at the supercomputer and pulled up live camera feeds of all 16 working NASA satellites orbiting around Earth. Cynthia grabbed more chairs and sat down with Alina and Leah. Leah pulled cables out of her robot body and plugged herself into the supercomputer. She now had full access to all 16 NASA satellites.

Leah looked at Alina and said, "I need you to focus all your power into me, then I'll send it through the satellites."

"Okay, I'll give you everything I've got, hope you can handle it." Alina affirmed.

"So do I," Lead admitted worriedly.

Alina closed her eyes and began concentrating. She thought deeply about Von's memories of his battles against the rock monsters. She specifically focused on Von's powers and how he absorbed negative energy from his enemies. Then she reversed the effect, wanting to expel the energy out of the monsters instead of absorbing it. She truly believed she could accomplish this, which was crucial to the effectiveness of a Believer's power.

Leah, however, was having trouble channeling Alina's power through 16 satellites. She was cringing in pain, trying to use her own power to amplify the effect, but it wasn't enough. Cynthia also had her eyes closed and was using her powers to watch the monsters on Earth to see if Alina and Leah's efforts had any effect. Most of Earth was unaffected, but Cynthia saw something promising in one city under a satellite. The rock monsters had stopped attacking and looked like they were having a seizure.

Leah and Alina finally asked for help and Cynthia knew exactly what to do. She placed one hand on Leah's back and her other hand on Alina's back, then she used her energy to increase their powers ten-fold. Leah and Alina's eyes suddenly opened with a bright golden light shining outward. Alina and Leah felt overwhelmed with power and screamed as they channeled everything into the satellites. Within seconds, all 16 satellites were blasting out Alina's power. Rock monsters all over the world halted and began shaking uncontrollably, but Cynthia knew it wasn't enough.

"Leah! You're the focal point! We're giving you all our power! Take control of it and destroy those monsters now!"

"Aaaaahh!!!!!" Leah cried out in pain and her eyes became ruby red, flashing repeatedly like a strobe light. The supercomputer's circuits fried, and sparks shot out. The satellites doubled their energy output and black smoke burst out of all the rock monsters. The black smoke slowly rose into the sky and dispersed...the threat was finally over.

All NASA personnel cheered in ecstasy as they realized the world was saved. Cynthia and Alina were overjoyed and gave each other a hug. Leah smiled and then fell off her chair. Dr. Wang caught Leah and unplugged her from the supercomputer. Cynthia rushed to Leah's side and used her powers to scan for injuries. Leah was heavily damaged, barely able to speak or move, but her eyes were open, and she kept smiling. Cynthia knew about the nanites inside Leah's body that can heal her injuries, so Cynthia channeled positive energy into Leah's body and enhanced the nanites. Leah's robot body quickly healed, and she gave Cynthia a thumbs up as a *thank you.* Dr. Wang hugged Leah tightly and couldn't hold back her tears as they rolled down her face.

"That was too dangerous! You could have died! Don't ever do that again!" Dr. Wang scolded Leah loudly but continued holding on to her.

After a moment, she stopped hugging Leah, wiped her face clean, and regained her composure. Then she said, "You were reckless, but also perfect. You did the impossible and I'm proud of you. You are every bit the child of Jerry and Cynthia, they raised you well."

Cynthia appreciated her words and acknowledged her, "Thank you Dr. Wang, but you are very important too. You created a robot body for Leah, and we couldn't have done any of this without you. In my eyes, you are Leah's godmother and part of our family."

Dr. Wang was speechless, and Alina nodded in agreement, then Leah sat up and gave Dr. Wang a hug. Dr. Wang silently wept, then Alina and Cynthia also hugged her, and she bawled, "I've never had a family like this before...thank you."

Chapter 25:
SACRIFICE

"THE TIME HAS COME." THE SUN PROCLAIMED.

"What do you mean?" Jerry angrily replied, "We stopped the asteroid and saved Earth!"

"I'm sorry, Jerry, but the asteroid sent by the darkness was only the first threat."

"How can that be? You promised me peace and I finally have it! What else do I have to fight against?

"Me...I am the final threat...I am the end of all life on Earth." The sun decreed.

"What? Why?" Jerry asked with disbelief.

"As you saw in outer space, I am constantly being attacked by the darkness. It slowly attempts to conquer and engulf me. Every several million years, I have to release a massive solar flare to push the darkness away." The sun explained.

"What's so bad about a solar flare?" Jerry wondered.

"Normally, my solar flares are small and only cause minor issues for Earth. But I've been using weaker measures to keep the darkness at bay for as long as I could. Now I must take a stronger stance or risk death, causing a supernova that would destroy our galaxy. Unfortunately, the asteroid's negative energy weakened Earth's atmosphere and magnetic field, all of which shield the earth. Therefore, my next solar flare will annihilate all life on Earth...unless you protect it."

The sun had just finished speaking to Jerry telepathically. Jerry was shocked, frustrated, and overwhelmed, so he took a moment to let everything sink in. He thought about history and realized that maybe the dinosaurs were wiped out in the same way 65 million years ago. Now it was happening all over again, but this time Earth had a chance. Jerry became invigorated and his mind began racing, trying to find ways to save the world. Their conversation ended because the sun had faith in Jerry, hoping he could make a difference. If Jerry could stop the massive solar flare from hitting Earth, everyone would be saved.

Jerry was meditating on the grass, strategizing about the upcoming solar flare event, when Cynthia suddenly appeared next to him. Cynthia was thrilled about their NASA victory and saving Earth; she was dying to tell Jerry all about it. When Jerry stopped meditating and opened his eyes, he saw her beauty radiating as the sun's rays shined upon her. Cynthia was wearing her long, lavender doctor's lab coat, which reminded him of their wedding day. Jerry's mind became flooded with memories & emotions, and he burst into tears.

Cynthia instantly hugged Jerry and sensed something was terribly wrong. She comforted him while using her powers to read his mind and heart. Within seconds, Cynthia gasped and sobbed too. She couldn't believe all their efforts today meant nothing...the earth was still at risk of extinction. After their shared moment of grief, Jerry looked into her eyes, caressed her face, and spoke.

"I have a plan, but I may very well die today."

"I won't let that happen! I'll help you!" Cynthia cried.

"You can't! One of us has to survive!" Jerry retorted.

"We can save the earth together!"

"It's too dangerous for you. I can sense that you used a lot of energy today and haven't recovered." Jerry reasoned.

"Who cares! This is the fate of the earth! I'll use my life force like you've done before!"

"Cynthia, this is different. We've never dealt with anything like this. I thought I was going to die with the asteroid, but this upcoming solar flare event will be far worse."

"That's exactly why I can't let you go alone! I'm with you till the very end!" Cynthia declared loudly.

Jerry felt her unwavering determination and took a deep breath, realizing he couldn't convince her to stay behind. Then he gave her a warm hug and agreed.

Afterward, Cynthia looked into his eyes, caressed his face, and said, "You saved the world from a big rock. The girls and I saved the world from a bunch of small rocks. Now you and I can save the world one last time...together."

They both smiled and shared a passionate kiss, as if it was their last precious moment on Earth. They thought about asking other Believers for help, but they knew all the Believers either spent too much energy already or did not have the right powers needed to stop the solar flare. This final challenge felt like their last date together, so they silenced their cellphones. They wanted to go out on their own terms without any outside interference.

Jerry & Cynthia stood up, held each other's hand, and created a green forcefield around themselves. This forcefield would protect them from dangerous elements and help them survive in space. After taking a deep breath, they jumped up and shot into the sky like a rocket. Within seconds they were floating above Earth in space.

They couldn't believe how quiet and peaceful it was, staring at the moon and stars around Earth. Then they realized how serene and romantic this would be under normal circumstances. Cynthia wanted to feel lucky and special, but only felt sadness and impending doom. Jerry, however, felt enraged! All he wanted was to live happily ever after with family and friends, but the darkness' conflict with the sun was threatening everything he loved. Jerry wanted to protect the earth from the solar flare and prove to the darkness that it couldn't win, that it held no power over Earth. Cynthia felt Jerry's emotions and became invigorated.

With newfound motivation, their energy exploded outward, creating a green umbrella that stretched for miles; it was large enough to cover half the earth! They hoped the solar flare would act like rain and fall onto and around their umbrella, just narrowly missing the earth.

They both looked to the stars and felt a massive wave of invisible energy rushing towards them. They braced for impact and the solar flare hit them like a train! Jerry and Cynthia were both violently pushed back! Their green umbrella began cracking and was about to break!

Jerry wanted Cynthia to leave and save herself, but she kept her promise and began using her life force. The green umbrella was temporarily restored, but Cynthia was dying. Jerry could feel her life energy burning away at rapid speed...Jerry knew she wouldn't survive if this continued. Jerry begged her again to leave, but she had an unbreakable resolve and refused to abandon him.

As the solar flare intensified, Cynthia's life force withered down to near-fatal levels...she was struggling to breathe. Wanting to save his wife and protect Earth, Jerry erupted into a fiery phoenix! His body transformed into pure fire, then he fused with Cynthia, completely enveloped her body, and instantly healed her. She felt relieved and renewed, so she enhanced the green umbrella and continued protecting Earth. Orange flaming wings shot out of Cynthia and spread across the green umbrella. Her wings began absorbing light energy from the solar flare, further strengthening the green umbrella.

The solar flare soon ended, and the green umbrella faded away along with the fire surrounding Cynthia. She smiled with relief, knowing that Earth was saved, but then she suddenly felt empty, as if she had lost something important to her. When she looked around for Jerry, he wasn't there. Cynthia began to freak out and frantically searched the sky and space but found nothing. She flew downward and scanned the ground, hoping he fell to Earth, but again found nothing. She quickly turned on her cellphone, hit the red PANIC button, and screamed, "JERRY! JERRY! WHERE ARE YOU? HAS ANYONE SEEN JERRY? JERRY!!!"

***

Right after the girls saved the world with NASA satellites, all Believers began checking in via cellphone. Thankfully, everyone reported that they survived...except Jerry and Cynthia. Leah was not too concerned at first since she thought all threats to Earth were resolved. When half the earth became covered by a colossal green umbrella, however, everyone began calling, texting, and sending pictures. Dr. Wang wanted to use the NASA satellites to get a closer look, but the supercomputer was heavily damaged previously. Dr. Wang stomped over to the NASA personnel who were celebrating and angrily demanded, "Someone fix my supercomputer now!"

While NASA personnel were scrambling to help, Leah had the brilliant idea of using her nanobots to fix the supercomputer. Leah connected herself to the machine and sent her nanobots in. Within a few minutes, the supercomputer was fixed and ready. Dr. Wang thanked Leah, sat down, and began operating the satellites, trying to maneuver them into the best position to see exactly what was happening in space. The satellites observed the green umbrella and began recording data. Alina sat down next to the supercomputer, closed her eyes, and psychically tapped into the satellites. Using her sensory powers, she detected Jerry and Cynthia's energy signatures. *They were the ones who created the green umbrella, but why?* Alina wondered.

Flashing red lights and alarms interrupted everything inside NASA and all personnel panicked, reporting that a massive solar flare was about to hit Earth! Upon impact, many satellites were destroyed! Since Alina was psychically connected to the satellites when the impact occurred, she got blasted off her chair and fell unconscious. Dr. Wang called for medics to help Alina, and Leah became extremely worried about her parents. She tried contacting both of them, but their cellphones went to voicemail. Leah sent messages to all Believers, begging them to find her parents, but nobody answered...everyone was anxiously watching the green umbrella in the sky, knowing it was the only thing protecting Earth from devastation.

After a few minutes, the solar flare ended, and the green umbrella vanished. The earth was saved again, but nobody was happy about it. They were all confused and speechless. Earth faced two extinction-level events back-to-back, yet the most powerful governments in the world only knew about the first event and failed to prevent the second event. 99.9% of humanity was useless and unable to help...everyone owed their lives to Jerry & Cynthia.

All the Believers' cellphones suddenly received the shocking emergency message from Cynthia, asking where Jerry was. Alina woke up to everyone asking questions, making phone calls, and doing everything to find Jerry. Von woke up as well and called Alina from her therapy office, asking what happened to Jerry. The Believers' hearts sank, fearing the worst about Jerry's fate. They all thought it was a miracle that Cynthia survived, but maybe Jerry didn't. Blake and Mr. Cream tried to be positive and boost everyone's morale, but it didn't work.

Cynthia was losing her mind and couldn't stop screaming. Everyone called her cellphone, and she answered every time, hoping for good news, but only heard more questions and no solutions. When she saw Jerry's parents calling, however, she broke down and fell to her knees, crying endlessly.

How can I tell them that their son is dead? I was supposed to help him, but I only got in his way! He protected me and the earth! He sacrificed himself to save me! I got him killed!

Cynthia uncontrollably grieved, feeling lonelier than ever before. She felt like her heart and soul had been ripped out of her body. She couldn't answer Jerry's parents nor any more phone calls.

Leah couldn't sit around and do nothing, so she told Dr. Wang to find Cynthia using the satellites. Dr. Wang protested, assuming that all the satellites were destroyed by the solar flare, but she quickly discovered that one satellite was still functional! Leah connected herself to the supercomputer, then found Cynthia through her cellphone. Lastly, Leah streamed the satellite feed live on the internet for everyone to see. She even typed captions on the bottom of the screen and narrated, explaining who Jerry and Cynthia were. She wanted everyone to know who saved the world and sacrificed everything for them. Governments, social media, and news companies swiftly found the live stream and shared it everywhere, putting it on TV and radio stations too.

***

Cynthia didn't know what to do and kept crying, until she felt a soothing warmth pass over her...it felt familiar. She stopped crying, took a deep breath, and focused her power. After a short moment, she gasped and remembered what happened to Dr. Diaz when Inferno killed him...his energy was dispersed everywhere. This time the same thing happened to Jerry! Cynthia could feel Jerry's warm energy all around her, as if Jerry himself was trying to comfort her.

Cynthia knew what she had to do, and she had to act fast. She sent a desperate message to all Believers around the world, begging them to lend all their power to her. Afterward, she silenced her phone, placed it on the ground next to her, and prayed to God.

"Jerry has done everything to help the world, never asking for anything in return. He loved and protected friends, family, strangers, plants, animals, everything, and everyone on Earth. He sacrificed himself to save us all. Now I can feel his energy, it's everywhere, all around me. I think I can save him, but I need your help. I've never asked for anything before, always being told to be strong and solve my own problems without asking God. But this is life and death, something no mortal should have power over. I am begging for your permission and aid...please help me save Jerry's life."

Unknown to Cynthia, billions of people around the world were watching her prayer from the satellite feed on the internet. Everyone felt her genuine love & care and prayed too. Across the globe, people of all shapes, sizes, colors, and cultures were asking their gods, friends, families, and strangers to help save Jerry Miller. They offered anything and everything they could, a truly powerful gesture from most of mankind to save one soul.

All Believers concentrated upon Cynthia, trying to donate their powers to her. Believers were taking a huge risk by releasing their powers. They were unsure if their powers would return to them afterward. Most Believers used their powers for their own livelihood, obtaining jobs and building a lifestyle around their powers. Believers also used their powers to uphold their principles & ideals, helping those in need and making the world a better place. And worst of all, what if it didn't work?

Cynthia could feel everyone's powers flowing into her, along with their emotions. Cynthia felt the Believer's complicated & shared feelings of guilt, relief, happiness, despair, and hope. She knew the sacrifice everyone was making. But she also felt something else completely unexpected...the energy and prayers of billions of people. She felt overwhelming support, honor, appreciation, and POWER! It took all her concentration and will to contain it! Her body radiated like a star, glowing bright enough to be seen from outer space.

She carefully focused everyone's powers & energy and executed her theoretical process step-by-step. First, she scanned the globe to find all the energy, essence, and memories of Jerry. Then she pulled it all together into a green magical coffin. Next, she gathered molecules from the area around her and used them to form a new body for Jerry. Lastly, she combined everyone's powers, including her own, and inserted them into the green magical coffin.

The coffin was now bursting with everything inside it, combusting like an overpowered engine, and Cynthia did everything to hold it in. She needed time to combine it all safely into Jerry's body, to bring him back to life, but it was like a ticking time bomb seconds away from exploding and losing everything.

As the energy surged and crackled violently, Cynthia desperately yelled out, "What's the point of belief if we can't save Jerry? He was literally the embodiment of belief! He believed in himself and everyone around him! His beliefs pushed us to incredible heights, far beyond our wildest dreams! And now he needs our help! It's our turn to prove ourselves! This is our ultimate belief, the collective desire of everything and everyone on Earth! This has to work!"

Despite Cynthia's greatest effort, everything inside the coffin was about to explode. As a last resort, she desperately hugged the coffin, willing to give her life to save Jerry. The energy was burning through the coffin, searing her skin, but she held on tight and screamed, "JERRY!!! Absorb all the energy and come back! You're the only one who can! If this doesn't work, then what are we fighting for!? I believe in you, we all do! So come back Jerry! You hear me? Come back NOW!!!"

3...

2...

1...

BOOOOOOOOOOOOM!!! The coffin burst with a flash of light, blinding everyone around the world watching the satellite live stream.

"What's happening!?" Everyone shouted while covering their eyes.

The world waited eagerly for the bright light to fade, wondering if their prayers were answered or not. When everything cleared, what did they see? What do you believe?

EPILOGUE

TEN YEARS HAVE PASSED SINCE THE ASTEROID and solar flare events occurred. The Believers saved Earth that day, but humanity was humbled & changed forever. People realized their flaws as a species and wanted to improve. They started working together to make the world safer, cleaner, and more welcoming for future generations. As a result, life on earth was thriving, better than ever before. However, there will always be certain events that are out of their control.

On a distant beach, two very special young adults enjoyed their time together.

"How did you make that sand castle? It's incredible!" The young man remarked.

"My grandpa taught me; he was the best! I can teach you too." The young woman replied.

"That's great! Let's do it!" The young man agreed.

The young adult couple began digging and preparing the foundation while discussing their plan to build a second sand castle. The sky was clear, the sun was bright, the sand was soft, and the water was calm. All seemed perfect in this tropical paradise.

However, something sinister was happening far away, something big, and it was heading towards the beach. An older couple sitting in beach chairs nearby noticed the danger first. It was a massive tidal wave that could easily destroy the beach and everything inland. The middle-aged woman pointed at the horizon and looked at her husband. The middle-aged man acknowledged his wife, stood up, and clenched his fist.

Surprisingly, the young couple jumped up onto their feet, ready for action. They both gave a thumbs-up to the older couple and the young woman heroically announced, "Don't worry Dad, we got this!"

Jerry smiled proudly at Leah and Jaxon, then he sat down and held Cynthia's hand. She was a bit worried, but she knew the young Believers had trained for this, and it was their time to shine. Jerry & Cynthia attentively watched their daughter and son-in-law fly across the ocean and dash head-on into the tidal wave.

ABOUT THE AUTHOR

Michael Moran is a 38-year-old man with a Bachelor's degree in English Education and a Master's degree in Educational Leadership, both from Florida International University. He previously self-published 3 editions of a 400-page gaming book called TIER: The Enhanced Role Playing Game. It took him ten years to write and revise the TIER books and sold over 1,000 copies. It also took him six years to write and revise the Believers novels, with the help of Scholastic, Authorhouse, classroom students, family, and friends. He worked as an English Teacher for 10 years and writes short stories monthly for Dungeons & Dragons players. He now works as an ADA Officer for Miami-Dade County government.

www.ingramcontent.com/pod-product-compliance
Lightning Source LLC
Chambersburg PA
CBHW070022260626
47159CB00005B/1924